A Map for Murder
A Mystery by 24 Authors

Published by
Patricia Rockwell

Edited by
Tracy Donley

Copyright © 2020 by Patricia Rockwell

For information, email Cozy Cat Press at cozycatpress@gmail.com or visit our website at www.cozycatpress.com

COZY CAT
PRESS

ISBN: 978-1-952579-17-2

Cover by Maria Levene
(www.marialevene.com)
Printed in the United States of America
10 9 8 7 6 5 4 3 2 1

This is the third in Cozy Cat Press's group-written mystery series. Each author below was charged with writing a chapter and then sending it to the next author on the list, not knowing where that author would take the story.

Chapters and Authors in Order of Writing

Dedicated to all cozy mystery readers everywhere

Chapter 1 (*by Lane Buckman*)

Molly rolled over and pawed for the ringing cellphone on her nightstand, squinting at the bright screen as she fumbled to swipe open the call. Bleary-eyed, she couldn't make out who the caller was, but it was four in the morning on a Saturday, and robo-calls didn't usually start until after nine.

"Hello?"

"Moll? It's Janet. I'm so sorry to wake you. I'm calling from—well, I'm at the police station in Shotgun City. I hate to ask this, but do you think you could come get me?"

"The police station?" Molly snuggled back down into her cozy bed and sleepily tried to reconcile her roommate's voice with the location she'd named. "In *Shotgun City?*"

"It's a long story. Merilee's in jail. I could call an Uber, I just . . . Well, I'm not sure they come all the way out here. Does Uber serve the middle of nowhere? I could—"

"No, no," Molly interrupted. "I'm coming. I'll be there in . . . like forty-five minutes? Maybe an hour. Shouldn't be much traffic this late. I mean early."

"Okay. I'll be out front. I don't want to wait inside."

A hundred questions whirled through Molly's mind as she got up and moving, pushing her glasses onto her face and pulling on a pair of jeans. "Are you nuts? Wait inside. It's cold out, and aren't there—like—coyotes and snakes and things around there at night?"

"It's scarier inside with those creepy cops. Believe me. I'd start *walking* back to Dallas if I weren't so beat."

"Listen, let's just stay on the phone while I'm on my way. You can tell me how you ended up there and—hold it. Did you say Merilee is in *jail*?"

"Yeah. It's a long story."

Molly grunted, stepping into her sneakers and sniffing at a sweatshirt before deciding it was clean enough to ferry a friend home from the tiny town of Shotgun City, which lay about fifty miles northwest of the Dallas-Fort Worth metroplex. "I'm listening."

Over the course of the next hour, and even after Janet was safely belted into the passenger seat of Molly's ancient Civic, the story was still unfolding. They stopped at a coffee shop called Vern's—which was located on the town square in Shotgun City and, thankfully, opened at five and served piping hot coffee made by Vern herself. Once they'd ordered breakfast—two Redeye Specials—Janet finished filling Molly in on the details of what had happened the night before.

"So when will Merilee be granted bail?" Molly asked.

"She won't." Janet shook her head sadly. "They said it's not up for consideration at this time. And then to top it all off, my car had to die."

Molly chuckled. "Good old Cherry Bomb. She always decides to break down when you're far from home."

Janet's red Volkswagen Bug, affectionately dubbed the Cherry Bomb by the girls, was temperamental, but she loved it anyway.

"I tried to explain to the police that it was all just a huge mistake, and that we were only speeding to get away from those guys in Shotgun City, but

Merilee wasn't exactly her best self in the moment and she just kept making it worse. It was so weird, Molly. She was just . . . scatterbrained and couldn't focus. I don't know if she'd had too much to drink, or what.

"Anyway, when they did the pat-down, they found a 'suspicious baggie' in her pocket, and then they ran a check and found a warrant for an unpaid fine. It was a done deal. No bail." Janet shook her head sadly and stared down into the mug of coffee between her palms. "At least I got to ride to the jail with Merilee when they impounded her car. She was so out of it and confused. I was able to calm her down a little."

"So let me get this straight. Merilee called you to come pick her up in Shotgun City tonight after I'd already gone to bed?"

"Yep. I didn't want to wake you."

"And where's your car now?"

"I parked it outside the house party where I went to get Merilee. Then when I finally left the police station to go home, I had to walk back there, and wouldn't you know it—the Cherry Bomb wouldn't start. I pulled out my cell to call you, and of course, it was dead."

"Wow. This has not been your night, has it?" Molly said, reaching across the table to squeeze Janet's wrist.

Janet shook her head. "When it rains, it pours." She let out a long sigh. "And since everything in Shotgun was still shut up tight at three-thirty in the morning, I had to walk back to the police station. And then I called you from there."

Vern brought out two plates loaded with bacon, hash browns, eggs, buttered grits, and toast, and set them on the table.

"So what was Merilee doing in Shotgun City in the first place?" Molly asked as she loaded her fork with eggs and hash browns.

"It's all so strange," Janet said, biting off the corner of a toast triangle. "Merilee said she got a call from her uncle yesterday morning, and he asked her to come up here and help him at the bank. He needed something out of her mom's safe deposit box, but his name isn't on the card. Only Merilee's. I asked her more about that, but she just got really weird. I still don't understand what her uncle needed or why Merilee would help him out in the first place. "

"Is this the uncle at the ranch? Uncle Ray?"

"Yeah."

"I thought she wasn't speaking to him. That's wild."

"She wasn't. They haven't spoken since June died. And I think the guys she was arguing with were from the ranch too."

"Wait. What guys? Was this at the party?"

"Yeah. She called me, said she couldn't drive because she was too out of it, and gave me an address here in Shotgun."

"You should've woken me up. I would've come over with you!"

"I never imagined it would be such a big deal. I was still up when Merilee called. I figured I'd run over here, get her, and then tomorrow, the three of us could come back and get her car. Anyway, when I got to the party, Merilee was arguing with these two guys. You know that baseball cap Merilee wears? The one with *The Flying B* brand on it?"

"Yeah. B for Boyd—Merilee's mother's maiden name."

"Right. Anyway, one of those guys was wearing a shirt with the same brand on it. Their discussion got pretty heated. Merilee was so angry."

"She didn't tell you what they were arguing about?"

"Listen, she was angry and confused, and drunk or something. I couldn't get her into my car. She got into hers, so I jumped in with her to try to talk some sense into her."

"But she'd called you to pick her up!"

"I know! I'm telling you, she was *not* herself. Nothing she said made sense. Before I knew it, we were on the road, speeding away from there and Merilee was just ranting and talking nonsense." Janet paused and rolled her shoulders. "Molly, do you think someone might have drugged her?"

"Usually, people get drugged to slow them down. Sounds like she was sped up."

"Yeah."

As they ate breakfast, Molly found herself alternating between laughing and shaking her head. Every group has that one friend, and Merilee was certainly theirs. Always good for a story and always into something she shouldn't have been—which was probably why she always had a story. Merilee was perpetually into some kind of drama. She walked a fine line between propriety, in her pastel florals and twinset sweaters, and outlandishness, with a propensity to hop onto the backseat of any motorbike headed out of town.

Where Molly was a deep thinker and Janet was a stoic, Merilee was a free spirit. She lived in the same small, sunny building as Janet and Molly, tucked into a quiet, tree-lined side street in Dallas' quaint Bishop Arts' district. Molly and Janet shared a tiny apartment, and Merilee—who didn't need to economize as much— lived just down the hall.

"Merilee's in jail," Molly said, letting it sink in. "Did you get to talk to her at all before they took her away?"

"No. Not after we got pulled over. The cop made her sit in the back and I was up front. But like I said, she wasn't her best self."

Molly hummed and swiped open the browser on her phone. "Visiting hours start at eight. We could go see her before figuring out what to do about your car. You want to?"

"Maybe she's had time to sleep it off. Yeah, we could."

Slumping down into the booth, Molly pulled the length of her box braids back into the scrunchie she always wore around her wrist. "But then again, it's only six now, so we could just as easily go get your car first. Maybe the Bomb just needs a jump. If not, we're going to need to get it towed to a mechanic."

"I hate the idea of going home without Merilee," said Janet. "I wish there was something we could do for her."

"I could call my bother. I mean, even though he's Fort Worth PD. Maybe he can give us some advice to help her."

"Calling Denzel is a great idea," said Janet with a yawn.

"I'll get breakfast," said Molly, waving for the check.

The little town of Shotgun City was quiet early on a Saturday morning, so it wouldn't take long to get across town to the house where Janet had left the Cherry Bomb—but Janet, exhausted from being up all night—had fallen asleep almost instantly after fastening her seatbelt. Molly tapped the address Janet had written on a scrap of paper into her phone and made the short drive. But as the Civic's tires crunched over the gravel drive, Molly let out a long, worried sigh. Janet's little red Bug was nowhere in sight.

Not wanting to wake Janet just yet, Molly drove the block slowly, scanning for any glimpse of the car. After twice around the loop, she pulled back into the driveway and gently nudged her friend.

"Jan? We're here, I think."

Janet roused and yawned. It took a second for her to clear her head enough to focus, but she nodded. "This is it. Okay. Let me just get my keys."

"But Jan, I don't see your car."

"It's right . . . Oh." Janet's mouth curled under as she twisted to look up and down the street. "It's not here. I parked it right there on the curb."

Molly thought for a moment, and glanced at the old Victorian house, which was still dark inside. "It's a little early to knock on the door here, so maybe we can drive to the police station and see if the Bomb was towed?"

"Ugh. Back to the police station. I guess there's no choice."

Backing out of the drive, Molly glanced around at the house and thought she saw a hand move the curtain in the front window, but it fluttered shut before she could be sure. Her frown matched Janet's. "This feels weird. Or maybe I'm just tired."

"Or both. Doesn't have to be mutually exclusive."

Molly laughed. "Okay. Next adventure." She tapped her phone, "Google. Navigate to Shotgun City Police Department."

Two miles and the town's one stoplight later, Molly and Janet pulled into the parking lot that served Shotgun City's police department, jail, and courthouse—all housed in one building.

"At least you wouldn't have far to walk from jail to appear in front of the judge," Molly said with a chuckle as they walked through the swinging glass doors.

The young officer on duty looked up from the paper he was reading.

"Was he on duty when you were here earlier?" Molly asked in a low voice.

"Nope. There must've been a shift change," said Janet.

"Can I help you?" the officer asked, putting down his paper and walking to the counter.

"I think my car might have gotten towed," Janet said, stepping forward and looking at the officer's nametag. "Officer Scott, is it?"

"That's right," Scott said. "Go on."

"So, I parked it last night when I came to Shotgun City to pick up a friend from a party." Janet looked at Molly and hesitated. "She's, um . . . the woman who's now in your jail." Janet motioned toward the door behind the officer that led back to the holding cells. "Anyway, there was some confusion, and I left my car parked in front of the house—625 West 8th."

Something flickered over Scott's face as Janet spoke, but he said nothing.

"Maybe I wasn't supposed to park on the curb there? Anyway, could you check to see if the police towed it?"

"We don't usually tow without tagging first," the officer said. "And I didn't hear anything about any tows last night. But I'll go check the books." His eyes lingered on Janet for a split second longer, then he turned to go into the back office.

Janet grabbed Molly's hand in a death grip as he walked away, and hissed, "That's one of the guys from last night! Merilee was arguing with him and some other guy!"

"So he's one of the guys who followed you and Merilee when you left the party?"

"Yes. I'm sure of it! But he wasn't in uniform. He was in jeans and a t-shirt with the Flying B brand on the breast pocket."

Both of them hushed as the officer returned, this time, in the company of another officer.

"This is Officer Bartlett," Scott said. "He'll check to see if we have your Bug."

With that, Scott sat down, yawned, and went back to reading his paper.

Officer Bartlett glanced over his shoulder at the young man, cleared his throat, and glowered at the girls. "I'm going to need to see some ID," he said.

"ID?"

"Yes, ma'am. I can't give you any information without seeing some ID."

"So you have my car?"

"ID, please."

Janet fished in her purse for her wallet, pulled out her ID, and handed it over.

"Janet Phillips?"

"Yes."

Bartlett looked between the photo and the woman in front of him. Molly suspected he was assuring himself that the long-haired, smiling coed on the license was the same person as the pixie-styled, sleep-deprived face of worry standing before him now. He smiled a little. "Your hair's different," he said, then laid the ID on the counter between them. "Sorry. Nothing new in our lot."

Officer Scott, still obscured behind the newspaper let out a little snort, and Bartlett glanced over his shoulder again. "You might try Duncan's off Church Street. If you did get towed, he'd have been the one to do it. He could tell you where your car is."

Janet put her driver's license back into her wallet. "Thanks," she said.

"Do you have a card?" Molly asked. "I mean, in case we need your help? If we can't find Janet's car, that means it's been stolen, I guess. So we'd need to report that."

"What? Oh. Yeah. If you can't find it, come back to fill out a report."

"Cool. Thank you," Molly said. "Oh, by the way, when are visiting hours? We'd like to see our friend before we go back to Dallas."

Bartlett glanced over his shoulder at Scott, who lowered his paper and gave the tiniest shake of his head.

"No visitors right now. You'll have to come back later."

"Later?" Janet said, her face beginning to turn an angry red. "Listen, Officer Bartlett—"

"Thank you," Molly interrupted, taking Janet by the elbow and heading toward the glass doors. "We'll come back later."

As they left the parking lot and turned back out onto the main street, Molly said, "It wouldn't do any good to argue with those guys, you know. It might end up making things worse for Merilee. Hard as it is, we need to at least pretend to be friendly if we want to help."

"You're right," Janet admitted. "But now I'm positive that Officer Scott was at the party last night."

"You are?"

"Yep. He knew I drove a Bug. But I never told him what kind of car I was looking for."

"Guess we should head over to Duncan's?"

"We should definitely do a drive-by, but I want to go back by the house where the party was, too. Maybe someone will be around this time."

"Good idea. I thought I saw a curtain move inside when we were there before."

Molly grabbed her phone and asked the GPS to take them to Duncan's shop, just off the main street of the town. It turned out to be a gas-station-slash-radiator-repair-slash-inspection site that also housed a tow truck under a corrugated metal canopy. Cruising by slowly, both friends craned their necks to see if they could spot Janet's red Bug. It was nowhere, not even behind the shop. The back alley and the fenced-in lot were free and clear, too.

"Well, it's not here, either," Molly said.

"Let's go back over to the party house," said Janet.

Molly headed back in the other direction, gasping as she made the left turn onto the street and approached the house. There, parked against the curb, was the Cherry Bomb. But something was off. The little car was decidedly closer to the ground than it should have been.

"My tires!" Janet cried before they were even out of the Civic.

All four tires were completely flat, making sad puddles of rubber under the weight of the rims.

"I only have one spare," Janet groaned. "When will this bad mojo end?"

While the two stood staring at the Bug, before Molly could wonder aloud whether they could use her spare from the Civic, the front door of the house opened, and a tall, skinny man in tattered blue jeans and a baseball cap, with nothing but tattoos in between, walked out.

"What's up?" he called in a friendly tone.

"It's my car," said Janet, pointing at the Bug. "I think I'm going to need a tow."

The man gave them a big smile. "Name's Duncan. Maybe I can help."

Chapter 2 *(by Joyce Oroz)*

Janet glanced at Duncan, then back at her car's four flat tires, and groaned.

Molly took a few steps closer to the two-story Victorian "party" house and attempted to engage the stranger in conversation.

He said his name was Huey Duncan but that they should call him Duncan—everyone except his grandmother did. Molly had questions: Had Duncan noticed when the Bug had showed up outside his house? Had he seen it here last night? Did he know Merilee? Had he noticed whether anyone from the Flying B Ranch was at the party? But Duncan didn't seem to know anything about anything.

Molly unconsciously adjusted her glasses—a little habit that Janet, who was a counselor and an expert on body language, had said indicated that Molly was getting frustrated. And in this case, that was spot on.

Molly was just about ready to dismiss Duncan as a twenty-four-seven party guy with nothing to show for his life except an impressive array of tattoos, when Janet dragged her attention away from her pitiful flat-footed Bug and asked Duncan if anyone else was at home.

"I don't think so, but like, I didn't check every room." He bent down to examine one of the tires. "You guys should call someone . . ."

"Ya think?" Molly asked.

"Who do you recommend?" Janet patted Molly on the back in a soothing way.

"Duncan's Towing, of course," he grinned.

Janet cocked her head. "A family business?"

"Yeah, my old man, and it's the only towing in town."

"We heard," said Molly.

Duncan laughed, and nodded toward the cell phone in Janet's hand. "I can punch in the number if you want me to."

Janet handed over her phone, Duncan tapped in the number, and someone at Duncan's Towing answered. He handed the phone back to Janet.

While Janet was making arrangements to have her car towed, Molly decided to try once more to get information from Duncan, this time lightening her tone.

"So, how was the party? I heard it was a gas!"

"Like, I didn't get here until three o'clock this morning. I crashed on the couch after working the late shift," he yawned.

"What do you do?" Molly asked.

"I work at the cotton mill in Hutchins. I'm the youngest foreman they got," he said, smiling proudly.

"So there was a party at *your* house and you weren't even here for most of it?"

Duncan gave a little snort. "Yeah, that happens sometimes. The guys come crash here and things can get pretty crazy. You know, small town, not a lot to do on a Friday night."

Janet ended her call and tucked her phone into her pocket.

"So this is . . . your house?" she asked, eyeing the lovely old Victorian.

"Grandma's house. She's away on business. Tupperware business."

Janet and Molly nodded their heads in unison. Somehow the image of an old lady dealing in Tupperware softened the tattoo impression.

When the Bug was finally secured atop a flatbed tow truck, the girls hopped back into Molly's Civic, and made their second visit of the day to Duncan's Towing and Gas Station on Church Street.

Sitting in plastic chairs waiting for the Cherry Bomb's tires to be re-inflated, the girls went back over the rest of their discussion with their new friend Duncan—who had loosened up considerably after he'd woken up some more. Molly had asked him if he knew any ranch hands from The Flying B. He told them he knew one fellow named Gibbs—who was a foreman there—but he didn't offer a first name, or any first-hand opinions of the guy. When Janet asked if Gibbs had been at the party, Duncan just shrugged his boney shoulders and said, "Dunno."

"Maybe he didn't know if Gibbs was there because he was asleep on the couch," Molly suggested.

"Or he's Gibbs's friend and doesn't want to get him into trouble," Janet speculated, pushing her pixy bangs out of her sleep-deprived baby blue eyes.

Just then Duncan Senior walked into the little no-frills waiting room to announce that the Bug was ready to drive. He ran Janet's credit card, handed her a one-page receipt, and Molly and Janet finally headed out of Shotgun City. They'd called the police station before leaving, but were told that they still couldn't see Merilee, so they decided to go home, get cleaned up, and then figure out what to do next—plus they'd call Molly's brother Denzel and see if he had any advice.

Molly followed Janet's car south back toward the city. The Civic was ten years old, but it was new compared to the Bomb, and she wanted to keep an eye on it going home. The girls watched their speed, not wanting to lay eyes on another police officer anytime soon.

The hardest thing to swallow about this whole mess was that they couldn't just bail Merilee out and bring her home with them. She was probably scared to death. This was one of those times Merilee must miss her mother terribly.

June Boyd Mason had died well before her time, and the circumstances surrounding her death had never made much sense to the girls. June, who was an avid yoga practitioner and ran five miles every morning, had fallen off a chair while changing a light bulb and hit her head on a countertop. It just didn't sound like June, and the girls had often pondered the incident, still in shock, even though it had been six months since June's death.

Molly was driving down the highway, lost in thought about June and Merilee and small town police departments when Janet called.

"Hey, Moll, think I'll swing by the coffee shop when we get back. Want anything?"

"I could use some caffeine," Molly admitted. "It's only noon, and this has already been the longest day ever. Hold on—what the heck? There's a cop behind me with his flashing lights on."

Janet looked in her rearview and sure enough, a cop was pulling Molly over. She put on her blinker, moved into the slow lane, and came to a stop on the narrow shoulder a couple hundred feet ahead of Molly. Even from that distance, she recognized the Shotgun City police car, as well as Officer Bartlett, who had gotten out of his cruiser and was peering into Molly's window.

Janet half walked, half ran to the Civic.

Bartlett saw her coming, stepped back from the car, put one hand on his holster and raised the other hand in a "stop" motion.

Janet stopped dead in her flip flops, feeling scared and a little dizzy.

"Ma'am, go on back to your car!" he called.

Janet pirouetted her body around and walked stiffly back to the Cherry Bomb, wondering what was going on. Molly had done nothing wrong. The girls hadn't been speeding. Then it dawned on her. Molly had a broken taillight! Could that be it?

As Janet intently watched from her side mirror, she finally saw Bartlett straighten, turn, and walk back to his car. After he'd pulled out into traffic, Molly pulled out as well, and started down the highway, giving Janet a reassuring wave as she passed. It wasn't far back to the city, and Janet felt better the moment they slowed to drive into their quaint, artsy neighborhood and parked in the shade of the trees that lined their street.

Janet, who had forgotten all about her coffee stop, rushed over to Molly's Civic and waited for her to climb out.

"I can't believe Bartlett followed us!" she said, red-faced. "And pulled you over!"

"You're not going to believe this," Molly said, locking her car. "Turns out he's not as appalling as he seems. He gave me some inside information."

"Huh?"

"Bartlett said he couldn't talk to us at the station with that other cop, Officer Scott, present, but he wanted us to know that he's working undercover."

"Undercover? That guy?"

"Yep. And that Officer Scott? Bartlett said he's a friend of Merilee's uncle, Ray Boyd."

"Seriously?" asked Janet. "So that's why he was wearing the Flying B shirt at the party. Did you tell him that guy tried to run me and Merilee down last night?"

"He already knew everything. And he said he was really sorry we couldn't see Merilee this morning. He said he has to—you know—act a certain way when the other cops are around. Janet, he's trying to help."

"Wow. I'm usually good at pegging people," said Janet. "I missed on him."

Molly smiled in agreement. "Me too," she said. "By the way, he has a little crush on you. He mentioned you like a hundred times in the five minutes I talked to him."

"Ugh," Janet said. "Well, I guess he's at least trying to do the right thing—like chasing you down the freeway to tell you that." She laughed. When she noticed Molly wasn't laughing, she asked, "Wait a minute. Why is Officer Bartlett undercover?"

"He's investigating June's death," Molly whispered. "On his own."

"Wow, that's crazy. So Bartlett doesn't think it was an accident?"

Molly shook her head.

"Good. I never did buy that story that she slipped and fell off a chair and hit her head on the counter."

"Bartlett told me not to tell anyone about his involvement."

"He surely knew you'd tell me, though. Let's get inside and I'll make us a pot of coffee."

They started to walk up their front steps when Molly stopped. "But Jan, you don't understand the worst part of it," she said. "Bartlett told me that the real reason they're holding Merilee in jail is because they suspect *she* murdered June."

When this met with silence, Molly waved a hand in front of Janet's dazed expression. "The cops think she did it, Janet!"

The blood drained from Janet's face. "Are you kidding? What does Bartlett think about that?" She unlocked the door and they walked into the hallway, down a few doors, and unlocked their apartment door, which was decorated with a festive fall wreath. The comforting smells of home greeted them—Janet's favorite perfume and Molly's famous garlic hash browns that she'd made the day before.

"There's more," Molly said, dropping her bag on the little bench next to the front door. "Bartlett said he's Merilee's cousin and he'd do anything to find the person who murdered his Aunt June. I asked why he thought it was murder and not an accident. He said he's found evidence."

"What evidence?"

"He didn't say," Molly frowned.

"Moll, that's not good enough. We need to know what he found." Janet stomped her foot, then felt foolish. "Well, this is serious," she said, collapsing onto the couch.

"I think it's time to get my brother involved," said Molly. "He finally made detective, you know, and he has eyes and ears in the police force in this area. He knows how these things work."

Janet nodded. Denzel was smart, loved his work with the Fort Worth PD, and definitely had contacts in the whole Dallas-Fort Worth metroplex. Maybe even in the Shotgun City area. Surely he could help them. Still, Janet feared for Merilee's welfare. She thought about the freckled redhead and wondered how it would feel to be locked up and alone.

The girls were startled by a sudden knock on the door. Molly hurried over and peered through the peephole.

"Speak of the devil," she muttered. "Janet, brace yourself. It's my mother and Denny. And they have food."

"Let them in!" said Janet. "Your mom's cooking is the best. And maybe we'll get a chance to ask Denny what to do about this mess."

Molly threw open the door. "Mom! Denny! I'm really glad to see you guys."

"You too, honey. We brought lunch." Beatrice Jones froze and took a long look at her daughter. "What's the matter, baby?"

"What? Nothing. Why do you ask?"

"I know when my baby girl is worried about something. I can feel it from ten miles away." Bea set her daughter aside and looked at Janet. "Hello, Jan," she said, shifting her attention to Janet. "Yep, something's wrong with you, too. You look exhausted. You need to eat." Bea bustled off to the kitchen.

"Hi, Bea," Janet called after her with a smile. Janet had always felt loved whenever she was in the presence of Molly's affectionate mom.

"Hey, sis," Denzel said, coming inside. He lowered his voice so their mother wouldn't hear. "I heard through the office grapevine about Merilee. Don't worry, okay? I'm on it. How's it goin', Janet?"

"Could be better," Janet said. "So you know about Merilee?"

"I have eyes and ears everywhere," he grinned, shifting the bulging grocery bag he carried to the opposite hip. "Heard she was arrested over in Shotgun City. But listen, girls. I know it seems like a big thing, but—"

"It's murder!" said Janet.

"It's *what?*" Denzel looked puzzled. "For a minute there I thought you said *murder.*"

"What are you kids talking so quietly about over there? Denny, bring me that bag," Bea called from the kitchen.

Molly, Janet, and Denny caught each other's eyes, each guessing what the other was thinking. Silently, they agreed they couldn't talk about Merilee or the mess she was in until they could be alone. Bea Jones had a tendency to buzz, even to strangers, about anything and everything. That was her sweetness, but in this case, it could be their downfall.

No impromptu visit from Molly's mom would be complete without a full-blown feast, and sure enough, Denzel began pulling hot, great smelling home-cooked food out of the grocery bag and setting the dishes on the table.

Bea and Janet added plates, napkins, and silverware, and they all sat down to eat. The girls hadn't eaten since Vern's Redeye Special early that morning, and they were ravenous.

Molly's phone rang before lunch was over, and she glanced at it to see who was calling. Janet noticed she took a calming breath before walking into her bedroom to take the call. When Molly returned a few minutes later, shaking her head, she casually reported that she had just talked to a telemarketer.

It wasn't until later, after Molly's mom and Denzel had gone home, that she told Janet about the call from Officer Bartlett, concerning a postmortem toxicology test that had been run on June.

Chapter 3 *(by Bart J. Gilbertson)*

Raymond Boyd tilted his Stetson back over his graying red hair and took a sip of hot coffee. He slowly closed his eyes as the rich, dark fluid swirled tantalizingly around his tongue and down his throat. There were many fine things in life, but nothing as satisfying as his morning cup of salvation. Some of the boys under his employ liked to have theirs with an assortment of flavored creamers and sweeteners. Not Ray. Dark roasted and black. He wasn't going to ruin one of God's best creations with that artificial swill.

What was with today's generation anyway? Walking around with their fancy smartphones and earbuds. What was so "smart" about those phones? A phone is a phone. You dial a number and talk to somebody on the other end.

Ray opened his eyes and looked around the ranch yard. A gust of wind blew some dust up onto the long, flat porch where he sat with one leg crossed over the other. He looked at his watch.

"Almost noon," he grumbled.

The boys were probably still crashed out from a hard night of partying. Ray smiled grimly to himself, remembering his younger days. He supposed some things never changed. Boys will be boys, after all. He took one more swig and set his mug down on the table. He stood and dusted off his jeans and opened the collar of his snap-buttoned shirt. Even October could be hot in Texas, but Ray wouldn't have it any other way.

Ray, or "Highway Ray" as he was nicknamed, hooked his thumbs inside his front pockets and strolled across the yard. He stepped up onto the bunkhouse porch, and swung the front door open. Sure enough, there they all were, sprawled out and dead to the world.

"Get up!" he said. His voice was heavy, like hard, cut gravel. "We got work to do!"

The boys slowly sat up, one by one, rubbing the sleep out of their eyes, grumbling at the displeasure of having been so rudely awakened.

"Come on! Quit laying around, now. You're all runnin' late as it is."

"But, boss, it's Saturday morning," Jax—Ray's new hire—said.

"You must've partied a bit too hard last night, son. Morning has come and gone. The day's half spent already," Ray said.

Jax glanced over with disdain. "It's our weekend," he said in a low voice.

The room grew quiet as the others stopped what they were doing and watched Ray slowly walk in Jax's direction. On his face was a grin that matched his voice. "Oh, that's right," he said. "You're new here, aren't you?"

Jax looked around, noticing everyone's eyes on him, then looked back up at Ray, who was standing right in front of him now. He slowly gulped and nodded his head.

"Well, I'll tell you what, then." Ray bent down, his hands on his knees, and looked Jax in the eye. "Since I'm in such a good mood today, I'm gonna cut you a little slack."

Jax swallowed—Ray's cigarette and coffee breath washing over him—and opened his mouth to say something, but then Ray continued on.

"I think I'll give you a choice." Ray straightened. "Option one, you can quit complaining, get yourself dressed and out on the south plain for fence repairs like everybody else. Or, option two, I'll beat the ever-loving stuffin' out of you, and then send you out to the south plain for fence repairs anyway. What do you say?"

Jax's face clouded over.

"Don't look so gloomy, kid," Ray said. "It's a fair choice. So what's it gonna be?"

"Option one?" Jax said.

Ray smiled again and slapped Jax hard on the shoulder. "Good choice. Now get going. Day's wasting."

Ray turned and walked out of the bunkhouse, and there was a collective sigh of relief.

Another man, taller and wearing all black, stepped forward. "You all heard him. Get dressed and grab your gear. Some of the herd broke through the fence line last night. I want Johnnie, Rich, Tim, and PJ to round up the cattle. The rest of you gents will repair the fence where they broke through. We good?"

All heads nodded.

"Gibbs, what about breakfast?" one of the ranch hands asked.

"Stella's put out some biscuits and bacon by the kitchen door for you all to grab on the way out. But daylight's burning, so move it!" Gibbs said.

As they filtered out of the room, Gibbs made his way over to Jax who was still shaken from his confrontation with Ray.

"He really must be in a good mood today," Gibbs said.

"That was him in a good mood?"

Gibbs nodded. "Yeah. Normally, if anyone crosses him like that, he just knocks their block off and thinks nothing of it. So either he's in a good mood, or he owes you something fierce."

Jax pulled on his boots. "Well, he certainly does have a way with words."

"That's why they call him Highway Ray. Because it's his way, or the highway. Welcome to the Flying B, kid." Gibbs smiled, turned, and walked out of the bunk house, the screen door slamming shut behind him.

Jax finished dressing and grabbed his gear. He had about head out to join the others when another man burst into the room, a harried look on his youthful face.

"Ricky, where've you been?" Jax said. "You're lucky the boss didn't notice you were missing this morning. He's in a bad mood, too. I'd steer clear of him if I were you."

"I didn't get it."

Jax froze and searched his friend's eyes. "What do you mean?"

"I . . . Well, I went to that party with you last night, remember?"

Jax nodded, keeping his eyes on Ricky's.

"And then I found that girl we were looking for, like we were told to."

Jax nodded again.

"And she was arguing with those two guys—I still don't know what that was about. Did the boss send them there too?"

"Ricky, what are you talking about?" Jax asked, exasperated.

"Oh, that's right. You didn't see that part. She was talking to that guy Scott and some other guy."

"Who?"

"I've seen them here at the ranch before, talking to the boss. That Mary Beth seemed pretty upset after they left, and then you came over, and then you and her had that argument out front, just like we planned . . . you know, to keep her outside, while I looked for it."

Jax grabbed Ricky by the shoulders and gave him a shake. "First, the girl's name is *Merilee*. Not Mary Beth! And enough with the recap already! I was there. I know what happened. Tell me what happened *after* all of that. The last thing I remember is that I went back into the house to find you, but you were gone. What happened then?"

"That's funny, because I went back outside to find *you*." Ricky smiled at this, but when he noticed the impatient look on Jax's face, he quickly continued. "Well, that Merilee saw me and came up to me yelling all sorts of terrible words. She was hammered. I don't know what you told her, but she was pretty miffed about something. She pushed me. And I mean hard, too. She pushed me down to the ground and then stormed off with her friend," Ricky said. "They got into their car. Then I saw Scott and that other guy go after them. They all went flying out of there. Well, I didn't want to lose her and I didn't know where you were, so I hotwired a red Volkswagen Bug and followed them. I would've caught up to them too, but that car was a piece of junk, and then—"

"Will you get to it already?"

"Sorry. Long story short, they were going too fast, with those other guys bearing down on them. Then just my luck, they got pulled over by the cops."

"All of them?"

"Just the girls."

"And what did you do then?"

"I hung around out of sight until they towed Merilee's car. I have no idea where they've taken it or her. Then, I realized I was lost."

"How could you get lost?"

"I'm new here too!" Ricky said. "I don't know the area yet. I was so focused on following them, I didn't remember all the different roads we'd turned onto or off of, and I didn't have a cell phone or even a map. And it's dark out there, Jax! I spent most of the night just finding my way back to Shotgun City. Once I was there, it took me another thirty minutes to find the right street. By the time I parked the Bug back where I found it, in front of the big old house, it was pretty late in the morning. I let the air out of the tires, and spent the rest of the morning just trying to get back here to the ranch."

"Why'd you let the air out of the tires?"

Ricky grinned. "Seemed like a funny thing to do. You know, like my calling card. I *borrow* your car, then you find it right where you left it, but the tires are flat. Pretty cool, right?"

Jax released his grip on Ricky's shoulders and stepped back with a drained look on his face. "So, what you're telling me is that you don't know where it is, or who may have it?"

"It wasn't in the house. That's why I went back outside to find you. To let you know. That's why I lifted the Bug and followed them. She must've grabbed it on the way out the door and we just didn't notice it. Or maybe she didn't take it into the house in the first place. It might still be in her car, wherever that is. Or when the Shotgun City cops hauled the girl in, they might've taken it from her."

"Do you realize what a situation you've put us into here? We're new at the Flying B. The boss trusted us with this. I got a little taste of his bad side this morning, and I don't want to see it again. How could you mess this up?"

"Me? I was doing what I could, Jax. You would've done the same."

Both men stood silently looking at each other, hands on hips.

"I really needed that money, Ricky," Jax finally said. "If we can't deliver what we've promised, we won't get paid jack."

"Then we better find it—and fast. Before he finds out we don't have it."

Jax sat back down on his bunk, his face in his hands.

"And why were those other guys there arguing with Merilee? Did the boss send them, too?"

"Jax?"

"Shush. I'm thinking."

Ricky sat down on the bunk opposite him and waited.

A shadow loomed in the doorway behind them and a rough voice shattered the silence. "Still lollygagging around in here, huh? Glad to see you finally found your way back, Ricky. Have you boys brought me what I sent you for? Scott didn't get it. So you two better have it."

Chapter 4   *(by Christian Belz)*

Molly's mother slid the last of the dishes into the dishwasher, then stacked the containers of leftover food and placed them in the refrigerator. As usual, Bea had insisted on handling all of the cleanup. Molly watched as she wiped the counter with a dishrag, took one last look around, and then plopped herself into a chair at the sunny kitchen table.

The afternoon was almost spent, and Molly was getting antsy to finish telling Janet all about her talk with Bartlett. She wished she'd had an opportunity to talk to her brother alone, but Bea was always in the room, and Molly was too tired to think of an excuse to get Denzel off by himself.

"Now that was some delicious cooking," said Denzel, leaning against the kitchen doorframe and smiling at his mother. "I love that potato casserole you make, with bacon and cheddar cheese. You must have been working all day."

Janet nodded in agreement from the other side of the room. "That was some of the best peach cobbler I've ever had, Bea."

"Aren't y'all sweet," Molly's mom said with a smile. "You know, the secret of those potatoes is the sour cream."

"Guess I'd better get you on home, Mom," said Denzel. "I'm working tonight."

Molly wrapped her arms around her mother, giving her a hug from behind. "It's always the best meal, Mom, when you're cooking. I ate too much of that Chicken à la King. Just couldn't stop."

Her mother smiled, stood, and gave Molly a real hug. "You sure you won't tell me?" she asked.

"Tell you what?" Molly tried to keep her tone light.

"Tell me what's going on that's made you so stressed," Bea said, giving her daughter a look. "Mothers sense these things, you know."

"I'm just tired. Janet and I had a late night."

Bea gave Molly a skeptical look, but then she and Denzel collected their things and everyone said their goodbyes. Denzel hung back as their mother walked out of Molly and Janet's apartment, into the hallway, and whispered, "Call you later," in Molly's ear.

She closed the door behind him, turned, and bumped it with her backside until the latch clicked, then leaned back against the door, giving Janet a bright look. "Now let me tell you what Bartlett told me. Let's sit down, though. That woman wears me out."

"Molly! She's your mother!"

"Always has been, always will be. And she'll chase me to my grave." Molly laughed, and they took seats at the kitchen table.

Molly took a deep breath and started, "Okay, so Bartlett. He got hold of the files from the original investigation on June's death. Of course it looked like an accident, but they still had to write everything up. He told me it amounted to a small stack of files, which he's been combing through. One of the reports had a scribbled note in the margin referring to toxicology, but Bartlett didn't remember seeing such a report. He double-checked the entire stack, and there was no toxicology report in any of the files."

"How did Bartlett get access to the files, I wonder," Janet said. "I mean, I thought the case was closed. He appears to be just a police officer, not a detective or anything. I know he said June was his aunt, which is crazy, because Merilee never mentioned a cousin who's a police officer. This whole thing is so strange."

"He said ever since June died six months ago, he's been determined to find out what happened. He never believed the official report about how poor June's life ended. I told him we didn't either, for that matter. Anyway, he didn't tell me how, exactly, he'd put his hands on the files, but he must be pretty resourceful, because he also managed to chase down that missing toxicology report, and get this: it showed June had been drugged."

"Whoa! So it *wasn't* some random accident. Either she fell off the chair because she was drugged—"

"—or the whole scene was staged, and she never fell off any chair at all."

"And somehow, that makes the police think Merilee did it?"

"And why arrest Merilee now, after all this time?" Molly wondered. "I mean, it's been six months since June died. The case was officially closed—ruled an accident. But Bartlett's trying to get it reopened."

Janet tipped back in her chair, toward the window. Pink rays from the setting sun filtered through tree branches outside and kissed her shoulder. "I wonder if they—the other cops in Shotgun City—know about Bartlett's relationship to June."

"He's keeping it on the DL.," Molly said. "And good thing, too. I mean, that Officer Scott has got to be crooked—either that, or he moonlights at the Flying B and chases girls in cars down the highway on his night off. And after all, someone conveniently misplaced that toxicology report. Why? What are they hiding? The whole thing is fishy."

"Hey, look at this," Janet said, suddenly excited. She held up her phone. "I haven't been checking Facebook since we've been running around, so I didn't see that Merilee posted this picture yesterday."

Molly looked at the screen. It showed a photo of Merilee with another girl, both holding waffle cones. Merilee's bright green ice cream was likely her favorite, pistachio. The caption read, *It's been too long! Having treats with Justine.*

"Who's Justine?" Molly wondered aloud.

"I remember her from Frosty Freeze. Merilee and I worked there that summer back in high school, remember? It's over in Las Colinas. We had good times at that place. I mean, the customers were crazy and we worked our tails off, but we made a lot of friends and ate a lot of ice cream. Man, I loved those cherry flurries."

"Don't know how you can eat those disgusting red dots," said Molly with a shudder. "They're like squishy little plastic nubs."

"But so packed with flavor," said Janet wistfully. "Hmm. Wait, you met her once—Justine. Remember? A bunch of us got together at the shop on my seventeenth birthday before work. We had an ice cream cake and then went over—"

"—to see the Mustangs at Las Colinas! Oh yeah, I love that sculpture! Those horses are, like, stretched out in a full gallop, running. A pack of wild horses charging through the plaza in front of a high-rise. So expressive! You can see their muscles engaged and the strain on their faces."

"Chasing each other through the fountain," said Janet wistfully.

Molly nodded. "I love the way they make the fountain splash up at their feet so it looks like they're actually sloshing through the water. But, you were *such* a nerd, even then, Jan. I think you liked the museum more than anything else about your birthday party."

Janet gave a sigh. "I haven't been there in years."

Molly handed Janet back her phone. "So, do you still see Justine? Can you call her?"

Janet shook her head. "We lost touch years ago."

"There must be a way to track her down. She apparently saw Merilee just before she went to Shotgun City. Maybe Justine can tell us what she was doing there, and how Merilee ended up at that party—and in such bad condition."

"Ha! Yes!" Janet was eyeing her phone again. "Good ol' Facebook. Justine just checked in at Guitars and Cadillacs!" She smiled. "Should we?"

"Well . . . It is, after all, only forty minutes away. Let's go find Justine and try to talk to her."

"Maybe have some fun while we're at it," Janet added, hopping up.

Molly looked toward the kitchen window, where the early evening light outside was just turning twilight gray. "It's still early. We should be able to get in if we hurry. Let's go."

"On it." Janet scooted her chair back, got up, and started toward the door.

Molly touched her arm. "Hold up. If we're going out, I have to change out of this sweatshirt. I'd really like a shower, but I don't want to risk missing Justine." She looked down at Janet's feet. "And you might want to ditch those flip flops."

Ten minutes later, they had changed and hopped into Molly's Civic. A slight cloud of perfume surrounded them as they headed west on I-20 toward Ft. Worth, into the deepening darkness.

They soon approached the familiar brick building with its bullet-shaped trees out front. Cars were lined up out onto Bryant Irvin Road. "It's gonna take a minute to get in there," Molly said.

They drove around to the big lot in back. It was their lucky day—someone was just pulling out close to the nightclub's back door.

"They're sure leaving early," Janet observed.

"Our good fortune," said Molly, pulling the Civic into the open slot. "Let's get in there and find Justine."

They climbed out of the car and started toward the building, along with a stream of other club-goers.

"Could you take my keys, Janet?" Molly asked, holding out her key ring.

"Why? Planning to tie one on tonight?" asked Janet with a smirk.

"Very funny," Molly said, rolling her eyes and jingling the keys at Janet. "I don't have anywhere to put them." She held up her tiny purse. "This thing is cute, but all it holds are a lipstick and a pack of gum. I can't even fit my phone in here." She tucked her phone into her back pocket.

Janet giggled and dropped Molly's keys into her bag. "The lengths we go to in the name of fashion," she said.

Molly stopped suddenly and grabbed Janet's arm. "Wait. How will we ever find Justine? There are going to be hundreds of people in there. Did her post say anything specific?"

Janet grabbed her phone and scrolled. "No, just a check-in and a note: *Time to party*."

"Let me see that picture of her again." Molly squinted at Janet's phone. "At least we know what she looks like. Long dark hair. That eliminates all the blondes."

"And there are a lot of blondes."

"Uh-huh."

They walked quickly across the glittery concrete sidewalk, adjusting to the slow-moving crowd funneling through the doors.

"I think we should split up," Janet said. "We'll cover twice as much area."

"You read my mind. I'll go left."

Once through the doors, they shuffled in slowly with the crowd. Janet gripped Molly's hand as they were inundated by the pounding music, high-pitched guitar riffs, and chest-rattling drums. They waited a few moments as their eyes adjusted to the dim light. Once a small clearing opened, Molly slid out of Janet's hand, turned to the left and set out.

"Call me if you find her," Janet called above the crowd.

"You do the same," Molly called back, giving Janet a little salute. "See you on the other side!"

Molly squeezed along the edge of the bar, scanning tables, all the faces of the people running together.

A Bebe Rexha song filled the hall, the throaty lead singer of the cover band doing a decent job of channeling Bebe's energy. Triangular truss work crisscrossing the stage held colored lights, illuminating the band and spotlighting the dance floor. Two large spotlights rotated three hundred sixty degrees, passing a bright stream of light across every corner of the bar, making it easier to see faces at intervals.

Molly pressed her way through the crowd, craning her neck this way and that. She discounted all the men, blondes, and short-haired people, focusing on brunettes with longer hair. It was hard to make out faces in the dim light, but she scanned and kept moving around the floor to find Justine. There seemed to be a preponderance of black, red, and gray outfits, along with lots of plaid. And cowboy hats. Midriffs and short skirts. Tight jeans on both men and women.

After a time, Molly pulled out her phone to call Janet and compare notes.

Janet picked up on the first ring. "Hey, Mol, any luck?"

"Not yet. How far are you?" Molly asked, trying to ascertain her own position.

"About halfway around my side of the room," Janet said.

"Me too. Okay, let's just continue and meet up at the back if we don't find her." As she hung up, Molly glimpsed a swatch of long, dark hair and a slim profile moving toward the restrooms. Was that Justine? Molly's heart started pounding. She hurried across the floor until she'd almost caught up. "Hey, wait!" she called out above the noise, gasping as the girl looked back—and turned out to be a petite man, who grinned at her.

"Oh, excuse me, I thought you were someone else," said Molly.

The man looked her up and down, still grinning. "Want to dance?" he asked in a tone that made Molly's skin crawl.

"Sorry," said Molly, "I'm looking for my girlfriend." She felt her phone vibrate and pivoted away, turning her attention to her phone. It was Janet. "Saved by the bell," she laughed. "You won't believe what just happened."

There was no answer.

"Janet?" Molly said. "You there?"

The line had gone dead. She called Janet's number, but it just kept ringing. Molly continued moving around the club's perimeter, now scanning the crowd for both Justine *and* Janet. She developed a rhythm. *Scan tables. Dance floor. Tables.* She found herself bopping to the country beat of Maddie and Tae, wondering which one the cover band's singer was trying to channel.

A dark-haired girl wearing a red halter-neck crop top out on the dance floor suddenly caught Molly's eye. That profile could be Justine. Molly moved over the dance floor, started dancing to a Lauren Alaina song, until she was so close she "accidently" bumped into the dark-haired girl. The girl turned around. Bingo. It was Justine.

"Justine? Is that you?" Molly asked, acting surprised.

The girl's eyes narrowed. "Do I know you?"

"Not really. We met years ago. But you know Merilee Mason, right? I'm Molly, a friend of hers. She's in trouble. I need to talk to you."

They both stopped dancing. "What kind of trouble?"

"She's in jail. Please, can we talk?"

"Jail? What? I was just with her yesterday. Last night. I—"

"I know. I'm here with our friend Janet—you know her, too. We just want to ask you about yesterday. Can we go sit down?"

Justine hesitated, and Molly couldn't quite place her expression. A shadow of guilt? Justine finally nodded and started off the dance floor.

"Can we go outside?" Molly asked loudly. "It'll be quieter out there. I have to call Janet. I lost her in the crowd."

"Hold on, I'm here with my boyfriend. We have a table over there," Justine said, pointing. "You can come join us. Call Janet from there."

"I can't hear myself think in here. You're coming with me. It'll just take a minute." Molly took Justine's hand, and caught her eye. "Please."

Something must have registered with Justine, because her expression softened just as a tall blond in a cowboy hat and plaid shirt came off the dance floor. "Here's my boyfriend now. Hey, Jeremy, this is Molly. We're going outside for a minute. Be right back, okay?"

Jeremy nodded and the two girls made their way through the throngs to the back door. There was an open bench along the back wall. "Let's sit over here and I'll call Janet."

They sat down and Molly tried Janet again. As the line went through the ring cycle and then clicked over to voicemail, Molly scanned the parking lot. "I don't understand," she mumbled. "Why—" That was when Molly noticed an empty space nearby. The exact space where her Civic had been parked.

Chapter 5 *(by Jennifer Vido)*

Janet kept her eyes on the road, not that she had an alternative. The creep sitting next to her was in charge. Where they were headed was anybody's guess. For now, Janet remained quiet and tried to take note of the landmarks they were passing. If the opportunity arose and she could ditch him, she'd need to be able to find her way back home without the benefit of GPS, seeing as he'd confiscated her phone—which had rung several times before he'd switched off the ringer. Molly calling, no doubt, wondering where Janet was and why she'd deserted her at the club.

But Janet would find her way back somehow. And as long as she had Molly's trusty Civic, she'd be as good as gold. Despite the car being ten years old, it still had plenty of pep. Janet felt a surge of appreciation for the fact that Molly had always kept the car in impeccable condition. Other than the broken taillight, it drove like a dream—and was far more reliable than the Cherry Bomb.

Sizing up the twenty-something next to her in the passenger's seat, Janet wagered he was someone's henchman. He didn't strike her as smart enough to come up with his own plan. But then, Janet wasn't feeling all that bright at the moment herself. If only she hadn't fallen for his stupid con! She replayed it all in her memory. She'd been so excited when she'd spotted Justine talking to this guy at the club. But when Janet had approached them, he'd tricked her into leaving the club with him, saying that Molly was outside. So this guy was a friend of Justine's? Janet should have known better than to go outside with a complete stranger.

She looked over at the guy now as they drove further into the middle of nowhere. She watched him send off a steady stream of text messages, wishing she could get a better look at his phone to see what the heck he was saying. For now, she needed to pay attention to the road signs. The area looked familiar, but Janet couldn't quite place where they were in the pitch black darkness.

"Um, I hate to tell you this, but the gas light just went on" she said, giving him a quick sideways glance. "If we're almost at our destination, we should be okay. But if we're in this for a long haul, I suggest we pull into a gas station and fill 'er up." Janet tried her best to sound pleasant. No sense agitating him. He didn't appear to have a gun on him, but she wasn't in the mood to test that theory.

"How much money you got in your wallet?" he asked in a gruff voice.

"Funny you should ask that," Janet said with a laugh. "I'm a social worker, which means I have a heart of gold and empty pockets. If I had to guess, maybe five—if you're lucky, maybe ten." She could see in her peripheral vision he was trying to figure out how much longer they needed to go to reach their destination.

His phone rang and he answered it. Janet could hear an agitated male voice coming through the receiver. Her captor mostly just grunted by way of reply. But then Janet heard it—the person on the other end said "Merilee." She was almost sure of it.

As soon as the call ended, Janet decided to do a little digging.

"Personally, I like Google Maps for directions," she said casually. "My friend *Merilee*, who I think you've met? Well, she prefers Waze. Which do you like?"

"Quiet!" he hollered. "I'm sick of that stupid Merilee." Cleary, he was distracted, typing an address into his phone—but Janet's heart filled with hope. Now she knew for sure that all of this had something to do with Merilee.

"There's a road sign up ahead for gas," Janet offered. "Mind if I pull off at the exit? The last thing we need is to run out of gas out here in the dark. Wouldn't you agree?"

Now good and truly overwhelmed with the app, the young man barked, "Yeah. Get off at the exit."

The gas station wasn't far from the exit ramp. On the opposite side of the road, Janet could see the ramp to get back onto the highway. Good to know, in case she needed a quick getaway. She eased the car into the gas station. There were three other cars gassing up in the bay, which worked to Janet's advantage. If she spoke up, chances were, someone would come to her aid.

The gas tank was on the passenger's side, which would make it super easy for Janet to slip out of the car and get a head start before the bozo next to her even noticed.

"Pardon my manners," said Janet. "I forgot your name."

"Jax," he grunted.

What an idiot, she thought. *What criminal introduces himself when asked?* Luckily, hers did.

"Jax, would you like to pump the gas, or would you prefer I do it? Full disclosure, the cap sticks sometimes. You might have to jiggle it a bit and give it a hard tap. But trust me, it eventually opens. I love this car, dents and all, even with its idiosyncrasies. Molly's had it for years, and it's like a member of the family. In fact, I left her—Molly, that is—back at the club. You said we were going to meet her, but clearly, she's not here. She's probably wondering—"

"Get out and fill it up," Jax interrupted her, handing over a credit card.

Surprised, Janet took the card and got out of the car. She couldn't figure out whether he was being kind or just plain stupid—or perhaps they were in for a longer trip than five dollars could cover. She took a gander at the card and read the name. *Jax Paxton*. Sure enough, it was his own credit card.

Janet began to feel a bit more comfortable that she was not in grave danger. Perhaps it was better to use this guy for information and a free tank of gas, rather than to yell bloody murder. Janet, after all, wasn't the damsel-in-distress type, and Jax was somehow tangled up in this whole mess. He'd known Molly's name, he knew Justine—and what's more—he clearly knew something about Merilee's situation too.

In fact, as she peeked at him in the bright gas station lights, Janet was sure she'd seen Jax before tonight. Had he been at the party in Shotgun City last night? Was that where they were going now? To Shotgun City? This wasn't the route she'd taken when she'd gone there the night before to pick up Merilee, nor was this the way she and Molly had gotten home, but they'd been driving between Dallas and Shotgun. This time, she was driving north from Fort Worth. The more Janet got her bearings, the more she felt like Shotgun City was their destination. And that made her want to know more—about this Jax guy, about Merilee, and about whoever the voice had been on the other end of the line when he'd been on the phone earlier. She decided the best tack to take would be to get Jax to relax and open up a little.

Climbing back into the driver's seat, she said, "Thanks for the gas. I can rarely afford a full tank on my salary."

Jax grabbed the receipt from her hand and said, "Get moving. It's not far now."

"Just point me in the right direction. It's getting awfully dark out there. I hope we don't get pulled over. The left brake light is out again and it's like a cop magnet."

From the way Jax shifted uncomfortably in his seat, Janet could tell he certainly didn't like her mentioning the police.

"So, how do you and Justine know each other?" Janet asked, in an attempt to catch him off guard. She remembered back at the club, how the elusive Justine, who'd been talking to Jax at the time, looked up and saw her, then pointed him in her direction. She'd called Molly immediately, but Jax had grabbed the phone and told her to come with him if she wanted to see Molly. The rest was history.

"Justine's my ex-girlfriend," he answered, not even pretending to hide it.

"Ah, so she's the one who tipped you off that Molly and I were at Guitars and Cadillacs tonight."

"Pretty much," he said.

"I'm trying to understand, but it's so confusing. We were looking for Justine. She was apparently looking for us. Is that right? Why—"

"That's enough talk about Justine," he grunted.

"Gotcha," Janet said. "So where are we headed?"

"I know what you're trying to do and it's not going to work. Keep your eye on the road and your mouth shut," Jax ordered.

Janet surmised it was time to stop the Chatty Cathy routine and mind her own business for a while. There weren't many cars or trucks on the road. She'd seen mileage signs for Shotgun City, and every passing mile confirmed that's where they were headed.

Fifteen minutes later, following Jax's orders, Janet pulled off the highway and turned onto a dirt road, barely visible in the pitch black of night.

A moment later, they passed through an entrance to a ranch. Janet squinted, trying to make out the lettering mounted on the wooden arch welcoming them. When it came into view, she knew she'd been right. It had been a while, but she'd been here before. They were at Boyd Ranch—The Flying B. Merilee's family ranch.

Janet's mind raced with different possible scenarios of what was about to take place. She made a mental list of questions she'd want answered if she was able to find someone willing to give her information.

She thought about Merilee's Uncle Raymond— better known as Highway Ray. As a social worker, Janet had a knack for reading people, especially those with no morals or scruples. From her personal interactions with Ray Boyd years ago, he was that type of man.

There were no lights lining the long drive that wound further into the property. The twists and turns kept Janet on high alert, as did the frequent dips in the road. The last thing she wanted was to have Molly's car end up in a ditch. Somehow she didn't think Jax would be picking up the cost for a tow.

"I've driven down this road before in the daylight, but not at night. Kinda scary, if you ask me," said Janet in an effort to get Jax talking again. "I take it this is a social call. Am I right?"

Since his eyes were still fixated on his phone, Janet was surprised when Jax mumbled, "You could call it that."

Dust kicked up from the road causing a haze across the windshield, coating the car.

"Molly just washed this thing," she mumbled under her breath. "She's not going to be happy about this."

Surprisingly, that remark caught Jax's attention.

"I rarely wash my car," he said, looking up. "That used to tick Justine off. She'd whine about being embarrassed to drive around in a filthy car. Just one of the many reasons we're no longer together."

Janet just nodded and waited, hoping Jax would say more.

"Actually, her parents hated me too," he went on. "Said I was a deadbeat with no future. Can you believe they talked trash about me? Heck, they only met me twice. The first time was at their house, when I stopped by to pick Justine up for a date. I wanted to take her to the shooting range, but I'd forgotten my gun, so I asked to borrow one from her dad. He said he didn't have one. Likely story." Jax scoffed and looked out the window.

"And the second time?" Janet coaxed.

"The second time was when Justine bailed me out of jail," he explained.

Janet thought about how to respond to that. It sounded to her like Justine's parents were right on the money. Trying a different approach, she said, "Yeah, good thing you moved on. Sounds like that relationship was going nowhere."

"Exactly what I was thinking. We're better off as friends anyway. We help each other out sometimes. Take today for example. If it wasn't for her, you wouldn't be here right now."

"Oh, lucky me," Janet replied.

An array of bright lights came into view. The main house was an expansive structure situated at the top of the hill. The property was butted by a large lake on one side. In the daylight, Janet remembered, the view from the main house was quite spectacular.

"Pull up to the house. They're expecting us," Jax said.

"Who might that be?" Janet asked, curious to see if Jax would continue with the oversharing.

All she heard were crickets. Well, it had been worth a try.

The place was lit up like a Christmas tree. Janet, feeling suddenly more nervous about this whole situation, edged the Civic into a spot next to a sleek black truck with the Flying B brand on the side, careful not to park too close. With the car idling she said, "Well, it was nice to meet you. If you ever need a ride again, you know where to find me, or at least Justine will."

"Turn the car off and hand me the key." Jax was all business.

"Molly really hates it when other people drive her car. I'd better get it back to her."

"Hand me the darn keys. Now!"

Janet paused with her hand on the keys, trying to think of any possible way to avoid handing them over.

But she wasn't fast enough. Jax leaned over and yanked them from the ignition.

"Get out of the car." He slid a handgun from his jacket pocket. So he *did* have a gun.

"Lucky you! You found your gun. Where was it?"

"Move it!" Jax shouted with a little more force than before.

Janet's curiosity—even more than her fear—motivated her to get out of the car. She gently shut the door and advised Jax to do the same.

"Keep walking!" he poked the gun into her back.

"No need for force, Jax. I'm fully cooperating with you." Janet looked up at the house, and a rush of memories came back from the summer the girls had spent there. She could still imagine June moving around the kitchen, and the smell of cookies in the oven. The house was beautiful. It looked like something out of a western movie or a magazine. *Good Ranch-Keeping*?

"No funny business. Hurry up! We're late," Jax insisted.

"You may be late, but I was never told a time. I pride myself on being prompt. My family jokes I'll be early to my own funeral, as if that makes any sense. Do you get it? I don't. I think it's a rather odd thing to say."

It wasn't long before all that separated them from whoever was inside was a large well-worn door with etches and scratches from years of use.

Jax jammed the gun into Janet's back. "Open the door. Now!"

Janet reached out to grab the doorknob, and pushed it open. Holding her breath, she peered inside, not knowing what to expect.

"Finally! What took you so long?" said a familiar voice.

Chapter 6 *(by Liz Graham)*

"Merilee was wild last night, more so than I've ever seen her." Justine and Molly pushed their way through crowds still flooding into the busy bar, until finally, they emerged into the back parking lot.

But Molly wasn't paying attention to Justine's chattering. The Civic was gone. She quickly glanced up and down the rows of vehicles parked outside. No, she wasn't mistaken. They'd parked close to the door, right in that spot that was now conspicuously empty.

A movement at the lot's exit caught her eye, and at last she found her car, but it was too late. The Civic was just pulling out onto the road, Janet at the wheel and someone else in the passenger seat, headed north. There was no mistaking the broken left tail light Molly had been meaning to get fixed.

"I lost her at the party—at that guy, Duncan's?" Justine was saying.

Molly's attention snapped back to Justine. "Wait. You were at that party with Merilee? How did you get home?"

"Yeah. We'd met for ice cream earlier. I thought we could go do some shopping after that but Merilee said no—that she was headed over to Shotgun City. Something about meeting her uncle? Anyway, she said we could meet up later and hang out. Then she called and said she was at this party, and I was bored, so I met her there. But at some point, I lost track of her and left," Justine said with a shrug. "Man, Merilee was a loose cannon. The weird thing was, she'd only had one drink.

She got really strange—grumpy. I saw her arguing with those ranch guys, and then I couldn't find her."

"We need to follow that car!" Molly pointed off into the darkness where the single taillight was fast disappearing. "Quickly! Where's yours?"

Justine shook her head. "My car? No, I didn't drive tonight. My boyfriend drove us here. You know what guys are like—can't be seen in a little pink Honda—God forbid—not manly enough . . ."

Molly ignored everything after the word 'no,' her mind racing. Where had Janet gone? What could cause her to leave Molly stranded here without a ride? And most of all, why didn't she answer her phone, or at least text to let Molly know what was going on?

"Okay," Molly cut through Justine's chatter decisively. "We need to get your boyfriend to drive us. Come on, let's go back inside and find him."

They would probably lose Janet with this delay, but Molly had to do something. *Anything.* Janet would never just take off and leave her here. Molly couldn't ignore the gnawing feeling in her belly: Something was wrong. Very wrong.

"Jeremy?" Justine shook her head. "No way he'll leave the club. Him and the guys are celebrating tonight. His best friend won a weight-lifting competition, and they won't leave here until they're kicked out at closing time."

"You'd let him drink and drive?"

"No, silly!" Justine held up a set of keys dangling from a large silver Bronco key ring, glittering in the flashing red light of the club's sign. "I'm the designated driver. It's the only time he ever trusts me with his baby."

There was no time to lose. Janet and the Civic had disappeared into the darkness by now, but if

Molly remembered correctly, there was a long stretch of road with few turnoffs in that direction. If they acted quickly, they might just catch up with her.

"Come on! You drive, and we'll follow her."

"What? Drive Jeremy's truck when he's not here? That's crazy talk! He'd kill me." Justine's hand dropped as if the keys had suddenly become too heavy to hold up.

"Will he come with us then?" Molly couldn't keep the impatience from coming through in her voice.

"I told you already," Justine said plaintively. "The guys are celebrating, they're not—"

Molly cut her off. "Okay, then, I apologize."

"Apologize for what?"

"This!" Molly snatched the keys from Justine and pressed the unlock button. A deep horn sounded further up the lot. It was a manly sound, and came from the biggest, blackest pickup truck in the lot. As she began to sprint towards it, Molly called over her shoulder, "You coming with me or not?"

"What? You can't— Give back the— Oh my gosh! He's going to kill me!" Justine raced after Molly and they met on the passenger side of the huge vehicle. "Don't you dare!"

"You going to drive this rig or not?" Molly said.

Justine firmly shook her head and planted her feet on the ground. "Not if Jeremy's not here with me."

"Fine," Molly said, running around to the driver's side. "Your call. You can hop in the passenger seat and I'll drive." She hauled herself up into the driver's seat, pressing the start button and putting the massive truck in gear in one fluid motion. Justine barely made it into the passenger's seat before they pulled out.

"I can't believe you're doing this! Slow down!"

Molly glanced over at Justine's ashen face, biting her lip. "Look, Justine. I'm sorry," Molly said, switching on the left blinker. "I would never commandeer someone else's vehicle. But this was an emergency. There's no time to lose!"

"I don't understand. Why are we following that old junky car?"

"Because that old junky car is mine—and Janet's in it."

"So Janet stole your car?"

"No! Someone's . . . I don't know, *abducting* her. We have to follow them!" Molly swerved out of the parking lot and pointed the beast's snout in the direction the Civic had taken, desperate to catch up with Janet. "Buckle up, Justine. This is going to be a bumpy ride."

"I can't believe this is happening!" Justine wailed loudly as she fumbled with her seatbelt. "You've kidnapped Jeremy's baby!"

"Technically, *we* have kidnapped the truck," Molly said with gritted teeth as they roared down the road. Unused to the sophisticated power steering— or for that matter, power *everything* in this monster truck—Molly had to focus all of her concentration to keep moving smoothly down the highway, which was getting darker and lonelier as the miles passed. "You and me together, Justine."

"He'll . . . he'll break up with me!" Justine's voice raised a notch higher. "Be careful! Can you slow down?"

Molly swerved to take the sharp curve leading out of town. She was pretty sure she'd seen a broken taillight up ahead . . .

"He probably won't even notice we're gone," Molly said. "Listen, I need you to try to get in touch with Janet." She tossed her phone across the cab to Justine. "Just press four on speed-dial."

Molly knew this stretch of road, because she'd just been down it this morning. They were headed toward Shotgun City, or at least to the countryside around the town. The darkness made it hard to know for sure. Unless . . . Molly racked her brain as she concentrated on driving. Yes, somewhere around here was Merilee's uncle's ranch. Uncle Ray. *Highway* Ray.

Molly shivered, remembering the summer she and Janet had spent with Merilee on the Flying B during high school. They'd been so excited at the prospect— had always loved hanging out with Merilee and June at the ranch—and staying there for the whole summer sounded like heaven. They'd helped out with chores and earned a little money to boot. Janet had bought a brand new pair of Justin ropers, and Molly herself had scraped her cash together to get the best Stetson she could afford. They'd talked of little else but the summer before them—living the American dream of riding the trails with the dogies, picnicking by the gushing brook, long starlit nights around a campfire with the handsome, clean-cut cowboys for company . . .

That was the summer after Merilee's dad, Joe Mason, had died, and everything had changed at the ranch. Running a place the size of the Flying B was hard work, and June, in desperate need of help, had accepted an offer from her brother, Ray, to come to her aid. Ray had moved into the bunkhouse and lined up the cowhands, and June, still deep in mourning after the loss of her husband, wasn't as involved as she should've been.

The girls took orders from Ray each day, and ended up with sore behinds from riding horses for hours on end, and the achiness of hard work that never left them that whole summer. When they weren't riding, they were sent to work mucking out the barns and digging ditches in the hot sun, all under the watchful eye of that nasty foreman. They'd never been dirtier or more exhausted in their lives. And the handsome clean-cut cowboys? Those weren't the kind of guys Ray hired. The Flying B boys were a motley crew who leered at the girls every chance they got—and Ray seemed to find that amusing. "Boys will be boys," he'd say with a creepy grin. Molly shivered again.

But if there was a bright side to the experience, from Molly's perspective, it was that her eyes had been opened to the ways of the world, and she'd discovered her own resolve never to let anything or anyone get in the way of her dreams or her self-regard.

That's why she'd been determined to stick it out and stay the summer. The girls had thought of calling it quits and going home early on. But the pay was pretty good considering they had no expenses, and they were collectively too hard-headed to give up. Instead, they learned their way around the ranch, got good at working hard and avoiding conflict, and came away stronger for the experience.

"She's still not answering. I think she's ignoring you." Justine glumly tossed the phone onto the wide dashboard and slumped back into her seat. "And you better have a darned good explanation for all this. I'm still waiting to hear the full story. And what does any of this have to do with Merilee?" Molly could feel Justine's eyes on her, although she didn't dare take her own gaze off the road ahead.

"Well, it's like this," Molly began with the explanation of being awakened so early that morning by Janet, and how much they still didn't know about what had happened with Merilee the night before that had led to her landing in jail. "And based on those Facebook photos, you were one of the last people to see Merilee. That's why we came looking for you tonight. We were hoping you'd have some insight."

"Hmmm," Justine said. "Don't know that I can help you much. Like I said, I lost track of Merilee at the house party. And she was being so disagreeable. She was fighting with those guys . . . I wish I'd just stayed home."

Shortly after exiting the highway, Molly slowed the truck as they came to a T-junction. Which way to turn? The Civic and its one working taillight were now nowhere to be seen—just blackness stretching away on either side. Molly sighed and thumped the steering wheel in frustration, then chose left.

After some time, Justine spoke again. "There's nothing down this way. Just the dump. It's a dead-end."

"Why didn't you tell me that when I made the turn?" Molly slowed the truck, looking for a wide spot to turn around.

"Don't you have a GPS tracker on Janet's phone?"

"Why would I do a weird thing like that?"

"Duh. So you know where she is," Justine replied with a huff. "So when things like this happen you don't get lost trying to find her."

"We don't normally need to keep tabs on each other. I mean, where do we go? Home, work, places around our neighborhood . . . We pretty much know where each other are most times." Except when one of them strayed outside the familiar circle. Like now.

"Look, if you're sure Janet came down this road, she's got to be at the Flying B," Justine said.

"What? Why do you say that?"

"Because like I said, the dump is down this way. The only thing the other way is the ranch. Thousands of acres worth. Right over there." Justine pointed in the other direction.

Molly turned the truck around—not an easy feat in the dark, and she was thankful there was no other traffic.

Justine wrinkled up her nose. "So we're going there? Yuck. Do we have to? Have you seen the fellas who work at that place?"

"It's been a few years, but yeah." Molly nodded her head. "I feel the same way as you about them. But my gut says Janet is here, and she's not answering her phone, and I don't know what else to do."

"Fine," Justine sniffed. "But this better be quick."

As it turned out, the ranch was only five miles down the road, just past the T-junction. The strong beams of the truck's headlights picked out the raised 'B' of the carved sign post, and Molly slowed almost to a complete stop before she turned in under the arched *Flying B* entrance. This ranch held such a mix of memories for her—wonderful times and awful times, and right now she wished she was back home with Janet in their cozy apartment, eating ice cream and watching movies. It seemed like a million years since the phone had rung at four that morning.

But there was no choice. Molly had to find Janet, and that meant going to the Flying B and possibly facing danger. And Molly had a sinking feeling that the mess Merilee was in and the mess she and Janet were in were somehow one and the same.

Chapter 7 *(by Linda Clayton)*

Molly drove slowly under the Flying B sign, trying to get her thoughts together. She went over the situation one more time. There was no way Janet would willingly leave her stranded at the club. It was crystal clear: Janet was in trouble. And the fact that she also wasn't answering her cell phone made that fact even more clear. Molly remembered how Janet had been sure to fully charge her phone that evening, so there was no chance it had gone dead again—and besides, Janet and her phone never parted company, and she always answered on the first ring. Molly had followed the Civic out this direction, and other than the massive ranch, there just wasn't much else around. She couldn't be sure Janet was at the Flying B, but it seemed like too much of a coincidence that in trying to help Merilee, they'd ended up back in Shotgun City—for the second time that day, no less.

Molly also realized that charging straight into the ranch might not be the best solution. She shuddered, remembering the obnoxious ranch hands she'd met back in the day and realized her fingers were cramping as she held the steering wheel in a white-knuckled grip. Her stomach felt knotted, too. Hopefully she'd find Janet soon, and this would be over.

"I'm not going in there," Justine announced suddenly. "And there's no way you can convince me to do it. I don't like those people, and I'm sorry I ever agreed to help Jax. I mean, he's an okay guy, but this is too much."

Molly glanced at Justine. "Who's Jax?" she asked. "And what does he have to do with all this?"

Justine rolled her eyes and let out a long sigh. "He's my ex, okay? When he told me he was in trouble and asked me to help, I agreed." When Molly just looked at her blankly, Justine continued. "Okay, this morning I got a call from Jax, asking me to let him know if I ever saw Janet—and this is the funny part, he also mentioned you. Took me a while to remember you—but I did. You were Merilee and Janet's friend—we met one time at the Frosty Freeze. Remember? Janet's seventeenth birthday party? We had ice cream cake and then we went to see—"

"The mustangs. In the fountain at Las Colinas. I remember," said Molly. "It's been a long time."

"It has," said Justine, nodding. "Anyway, Jax said he needed to talk to you and Janet—that it was really important. I wouldn't have done anything about it, but when you two came into the club tonight, I couldn't believe it. You were both there, and so was Jax! Then you separated, and I lost sight of you, but I saw Janet and pointed her out to him. That's all I did. I mean, what's wrong with that?" Molly didn't answer, so Justine continued, "I wouldn't have thought she'd leave the club with Jax. I mean, I thought he just wanted to talk to y'all. Except . . . "

"Except what?" said Molly.

"Except that Jax works here—at the Flying B. He just got the job like a week ago. And we know Janet came this way. And now here we are. So she must be with Jax. I swear to you, Molly, I hadn't put it together that Jax might be the one who abducted Janet. If he is, I'm going to throttle him!" Justine looked at Molly. "But Molly, if it makes you feel any better, I know Jax. And he may be a dope, but I can't imagine he'd do anything really bad. I mean, I have no idea why he'd bring Janet out here. I know he wouldn't hurt her."

"I guess we'll have to ask him when we find him. So why did you two break up?" By this time, Molly had pulled over to the side of the road to formulate a plan.

Justine sighed. "I don't know. Maybe I made a mistake. Jax is . . . well . . . sensitive. Kind of soft. He likes to read. Can you imagine, he even likes to watch movies with subtitles? Who does that? I like my men a bit rougher. Jeremy is tough. He doesn't talk much, though, and mostly likes to go to bars and drink beer."

"Sounds delightful."

"Yeah," Justine said, but didn't look so sure she believed it. "So what are we going to do now?"

"We're going to do this." Molly pulled out and wheeled the big truck to the right down a narrow dirt road. She winced as branches scraped both sides of the shiny black paint.

"Please tell me you did not just do that!"

"Sorry," Molly said, as she eased to a stop in the clearing. "Here's the plan. We're going to leave the truck here and scout out the situation on foot. I don't like the kind of men who work here, and neither do you—unless Raymond Boyd has taken to hiring upstanding citizens, and I seriously doubt that's the case. Since we have no idea what's going on, it makes no sense to drive in there in this huge truck, march up to the front door, and ring the bell. I have a feeling that wouldn't go over well."

Even in the dark, Molly could sense the astonished look on Justine's face. "Are you crazy? What do you mean by *scout out the situation*? You do realize these people have guns, right?" She shook her head. "No way I'm doing that. And I'm certainly not leaving Jeremy's truck here in the dark."

"Suit yourself." Molly opened the door and jumped to the ground. She dangled the keys in front of Justine's face. "But I'm taking these. Do you really want to stay out here all alone? It's awfully dark."

Molly was almost back out to the road when she heard footsteps behind her.

"Okay, I'm here." Justine stopped to catch her breath. "I'm probably going to regret this, but I don't want to stay in the truck by myself. What are we going to do now?"

Molly didn't mind admitting to herself she felt better with someone beside her—even a reluctant someone who talked too much. "We'll sneak up to the ranch and have a look around. We don't know for sure that your friend Jax brought Janet here. If he didn't, we may have to call the police. If he did, we have to get Janet out of there. But before I go anywhere near Raymond Boyd, I want to make sure it's safe. I don't want any surprises. The main house is just around the bend. If we stick to the side of the road in the shadows we'll be out of sight."

"I still think you're crazy. And it's scary out here," said Justine, moving even closer to Molly. "We have to stay close together."

Molly laughed. "I don't think we could be much closer. I can feel your breath on the back of my neck."

"Sorry. I'll back up. It's just that this place gives me the creeps."

Molly reached back and squeezed Justine's hand. "When this is over, and we have Janet safely back with us and Merilee home, you should come hang out with us."

Justine took a deep breath. "If we get out of here in one piece, I'd like that."

As they walked, Molly tried to remember the layout of the ranch. There was the main house, the horse barn, several other smaller outbuildings, and a bunkhouse for the ranch hands. And there was also a tiny playhouse at the back of the property. When Merilee's great grandfather had built the ranch, he'd also built the little structure for his children and grandchildren. Merilee had played there as a child, as had her mother, June. But over the years it had fallen into disrepair, and Highway Ray certainly had no interest in keeping it up. Molly smiled in the dark, remembering the times she, Janet, and Merilee had snuck off to the playhouse to hide out that summer they'd worked on the ranch.

An urgent pull on her arm jerked her back to the present moment. "How are we ever going to get across the circular drive?" Justine pointed at the house. "There are lights in the front windows."

"We're going to be very careful. And I may have a plan. Oh, my goodness . . ." said Molly, stopping suddenly.

"What?"

"Look over there in the parking area. That Civic is my car. That confirms that Janet's definitely here. And my quivering insides tell me she's in trouble. She would never have visited the Flying B Ranch voluntarily with June gone."

"There are plenty of Civics around that look just like that. Are you positive that one's yours?"

Molly used the flashlight on her phone to briefly illuminate the taillight. "See? Broken taillight. Come on. We have to find Janet. Follow me and be very quiet."

Together they crept across the porch, avoiding rocking chairs and empty beer bottles. When Molly stepped on a dog toy and it squeaked, both girls froze, listening for heavy footsteps. When none came, they clung to the wall until they reached the first of the large front windows and peered in.

Even as a teenager, Molly had been in awe of the Flying B Ranch. She loved the great room best of all. It had such character: old wood floors rubbed smooth by the passage of time and many feet, colorful pillows on comfy leather couches positioned in a semicircle on an intricately patterned area rug, and best of all, the massive stone fireplace. A tiered chandelier made entirely of antlers hung from the vaulted ceiling. The room was warm and inviting and Molly never thought Raymond Boyd, crude and rude as he was, belonged here. No, this room looked more like June. June, who'd lived here happily with her husband, Joe. June, who'd raised Merilee out here in the fresh air of the countryside. Molly felt a stab of sadness—both because June had left the world too soon, and because this beautiful place had been left in the hands of June's undeserving brother, so that Merilee couldn't spend time here anymore. Such a waste.

"This is amazing," Justine whispered, taking in the beautiful room. "I've never been inside the main house."

"It is," Molly agreed, scanning the empty room. "This room has looked this way forever. Ray had nothing to do with it. And speaking of Uncle Ray, he isn't in there."

"So what do we do now?" Justine swatted at an unidentified insect on her shoulder.

"We go around to the back of the house. The kitchen is there and also a little sitting room. We'll have a look."

They followed the stone path past oleander bushes—still blooming, even in late fall—and tangled masses of lantana. At the back of the house they climbed steps to a screened porch. Molly gingerly tried the door, and when it opened with a soft squeak, they stepped in and walked to a window.

"This is the kitchen," Molly whispered, cupping her hands to the glass. "Next is the sitting room." She peered deeper in, and her heart began thudding so loudly that people in the room might've heard it. And there definitely *were* people in the room. Janet sat in a chair, and two men stood in front of her with their backs to the window. Molly instantly recognized the lanky man standing with legs apart and his hands behind his back as Raymond Boyd.

"Yep. There's Jax," Justine said with a sigh. "I guess my mom was right about him when she said he was no good."

Molly watched in dismay as Janet shook her head emphatically at something and recoiled in disgust as Uncle Ray leaned forward, his face too close to hers.

Poor Janet! Molly wanted to run into the room and whack Ray over the head with something heavy, but instead she turned to Justine. "We have to do something," she whispered, picking up a metal gardening trowel and weighing it in her hand. Could she use this to inflict some kind of damage? Probably not. One small metal trowel against two big men who were probably armed didn't seem like a brilliant idea.

Justine picked stones out of a planter and handed them to Molly. "Could we use these?"

"What would we do with these? Those guys probably have elephant hides. They wouldn't feel a thing. I think we need to create a diversion. Maybe startle them enough to slip in and spring Janet."

"Well, why didn't you say that before?" Justine reached into the bag slung over her shoulder and pulled out a gun. Light from the window bounced off the small metal pistol, making it look cold and dangerous.

"For heaven's sake! Where did you get that?"

"Don't you have one? Every girl should have a gun for protection. My dad gave this to me."

"*No*, I don't have one. And please don't wave that thing around. Is it loaded?"

"Of course it's loaded. Now if you'll excuse me, I'm going to go outside and shoot it. I can't spend any more time on this. I want to get back to Fort Worth. Are you coming?" She sprang out the back door.

"Do I have a choice?" Molly yelled after her. She was barely off the porch when several extremely loud bangs shattered the quiet night. There was a pause and then more bangs.

Justine ran out of the darkness. "That'll bring those men out of the house. Hurry! We have to hide!"

They ducked behind a potting shed, but they might as well have stayed in plain sight on the driveway. The front door flew open and Uncle Ray and Jax ran down the steps, jumped into the black pickup truck with the Flying B emblem on the side, and roared away without so much as a sideways glance.

"Well *that* was strange." Justine tucked the gun back into her bag. "I expected them to come out of the house—but not run away."

Before Molly could say another word, Janet came running down the front porch steps and toward the Civic.

"Janet! Wait! It's me, Molly!" She caught up with Janet just as she was opening the car door. "Come on, Justine!"

Confusion spread over Janet's face. "Molly? You found me?"

Molly ran to the passenger side and yanked open the door. "I'll explain later. Let's get out of here first. You're already on that side, so you drive."

Janet nodded and got in, and Justine hopped into the backseat as Janet coaxed the Civic to life and they made their way down the drive and toward the ranch's exit. Justine managed to squeeze in a heartfelt apology to Janet for telling Jax who she was, just before Molly pointed the way to where she'd parked Jeremy's truck. Within a few minutes, they'd dropped a relieved Justine off and were headed down the road, back toward the city.

When they reached the highway, Molly relaxed enough to talk and quickly brought Janet up to speed about how she'd arrived at the Flying B. "When I saw you driving off in my car at the club, and you never contacted me, I knew you were in trouble."

"I didn't know what to expect when Jax made me drive to the ranch," Janet said. "We all know Raymond Boyd is kind of a creep, but I never thought he was a criminal."

"He sure took off like a guilty man when he heard those shots from Justine's pistol," Molly said with a bitter laugh.

"It wasn't the gunshots," said Janet. "I'm not sure those guys even heard them. Boyd got a phone call that upset both of them. He shouted, 'I'm on my way' into the phone, and they both tore out of the house. They completely forgot about me. And that Jax was dumb enough to leave the keys to the Civic in the bowl by the door."

"This whole thing is crazy," Molly said. "Why were you hauled to the ranch anyway? What did Uncle Ray want with you?"

"He told me there was something of his in Merilee's Kia and he wanted me to go to the impound lot and retrieve it. He said I'd be able to talk to the police and tell them I'd left my jacket in the car the other night when they impounded it. Apparently, the cop who oversees the impound isn't one of Ray's lackeys, so poor old Ray hasn't been able to get in there and get into Merilee's car. And Molly, you'll never guess who it is. Our friend, Bartlett! Ray said something to Jax about what a pain in the you-know-what Bartlett is."

"Way to go, Officer Bartlett!" said Molly.

"Heroes do come in all shapes and sizes," said Janet with a smile. "And you were right: Bartlett does have a little crush on me. That's why Ray sent Jax to get me. That Officer Scott told Ray that he noticed the way Bartlett smiled at me when we were at the station. So Ray figured I could sweet talk Bartlett into letting me into the impound."

"So what did you say?"

"I told him only the vehicle's owner and the police are allowed in there. Of course, he insisted I could pull it off, and then said he'd make sure Merilee spent the rest of her life in prison for murder if I didn't do as I was told."

Molly shook her head. "So you're telling me that he sent his little minion, Jax, to find you and bring you all the way back to Shotgun City so that you could get into Merilee's Kia? Boy, he's going to be mad when he gets back from wherever they went and finds you gone."

"I know," said Janet with a shiver. "But at least now we know that we can probably trust Bartlett. I mean, if he was one of Ray's men, he would've been all too glad to walk into the impound and get into the car himself, right?"

"Makes sense. I'm still not a hundred percent sure about Bartlett," said Molly. "But after all, he is investigating June's death. And he is Merilee's cousin."

"On the other hand, Merilee has never mentioned him, which seems odd. And Bartlett wouldn't let us visit her in her cell this morning . . . It's hard to know who to really trust."

Molly thought for a moment. "So whatever Ray is after is in his jacket, and his jacket is in Merilee's Kia."

"Exactly."

"Well, there's only one thing to do," Molly said finally.

"Talk to your brother, Denzel?" Janet asked hopefully.

"That . . .or maybe we could have a look in the impound lot ourselves."

Chapter 8 *(by Judy L. Murray)*

"I still can't believe they dragged you all the way out to the ranch," said Molly, as they drove on through the dark. "What on earth could be in that jacket?"

"I wonder the same thing. They refused to believe I didn't know anything about it, or that I don't have any more access to Merilee's car than they do." Janet slowed down as they approached the gas station where she and Jax had stopped earlier. She peered up and down the side roads, and finally relaxed her shoulders and took a deep breath. "I think we're okay. There isn't anyone following us."

Molly gripped the edge of the armrest. "There has to be something extremely important inside that jacket."

"I agree. From what I can piece together after overhearing Jax and Ray talking, this whole nightmare started when Merilee met Ray at the bank in Shotgun City. He needed her to open her mom's old safe deposit box. I think he snuck something out of the box and put it into his jacket pocket. And then somehow, Merilee ended up with the jacket in her car."

Molly nodded in the dark.

Janet kept her eyes on the rearview mirror. "We know that the police now believe Merilee's mom was murdered—or at least Bartlett does—and the postmortem tests support him. And that makes me wonder: Was there something in June's safe deposit box that incriminated Ray? Maybe Ray was holding something over her? My guess is it's either something he wants, or something he can't let anyone else see. Ever."

"I never have understood why Merilee didn't inherit anything when June died. Didn't you wonder why the ranch wasn't at least split between the two of them?" Molly tugged on her seatbelt.

"Absolutely. I guess I decided Ray got the ranch because he knew how to run it." Janet paused. "As a social worker, I see a lot of strange family dynamics, but leaving your daughter out entirely is pretty cruel, and certainly not June's style."

Molly shook her head. "No way. She and Merilee were close. She would've left her something."

Janet paused as she switched the Civic's high beams to low. "Let's face it. After Merilee's father died, June tried hard to make things work on the ranch for them. But for June, working the ranch twelve hours a day, seven days a week was a killer." She blinked. "Sorry. Poor choice of words. June needed help. Then Highway Ray came into the picture and everything turned ugly. They weren't exactly the Brady Bunch."

Molly traced her index finger across the window. "If Ray blackmailed June into willing the ranch entirely to him, and the proof was in that bank box, he'd be pretty desperate to get it back, wouldn't he? And now Merilee is the one in jail. He's the one in possession of June's estate. I mean, what if he was afraid Merilee would eventually contest the will? My guess is he has no intention of moving out of the main house and back into the bunkhouse."

Streetlights in town started coming into view. Within a few minutes, they pulled up in front of their apartment. A little porch light cheerily lit the homemade grapevine wreath on the building's front door. The two friends got out of the car and went inside, exhausted and glad to be home after what had to be the longest day ever.

"Whether we like it or not, if we don't figure this out fast, the case could slip through the cracks and Merilee could rot in jail," Molly said, rubbing her temples. "And those creeps at the ranch could come after us." She pulled her arms tightly across her chest and shivered.

"Can't you put your research skills to work and dive into Ray's financials?" asked Janet. "Maybe dig something up?"

"Are you crazy? I can't do that! I could lose my job." Molly thought for a moment. "I've got a better idea. I think we need to put Denzel and our friend Officer Bartlett in the same room and tell them what we heard. Denny can help get Bartlett to look at this case from a new angle. After all, he's been investigating June's death. He's Merilee's cousin, for heaven's sake! If he knows her at all, he knows she wouldn't kill her mother! Between the two of them, maybe we can even get into that impound lot and find that darned jacket before Ray does."

"Do you really think Bartlett will listen to us?" Janet asked.

"Hey, like Ray said, he likes you. And I saw him seriously looking you over this morning."

"Ugh."

"I know it's a longshot, but we have to try something. Right now, we're nowhere." Molly raised her eyebrows at Janet. "What do you say? You call Bartlett and arrange a meeting. Pour on the charm. I'll call my brother."

Nine o'clock the next morning, Janet walked into the Shotgun City police station and asked for Officer

Bartlett. The sergeant at the desk pointed to a wooden bench and asked her to wait. A couple minutes later, Bartlett walked into the lobby area.

"This is a surprise," he said, clearly pleased to see Janet.

"So they've got you working on a Sunday, huh?" Janet gave him a wide, bright smile.

"I've been busy lately," he said with a grin. "And law enforcement doesn't really recognize weekends."

Janet took a step closer to Bartlett. "I'd love to say hello to Merilee. Would that be possible?"

"Not just yet," he answered, a look of apology on his face. "But soon. I promise. Is there anything else I can do for you?"

"Actually, it's what I can do for you. I had quite a wild ride into the country last night, and I thought you should hear about it." She lowered her voice to a whisper. "It could affect your investigation into June's murder." She uncrossed her legs and rose to her feet with a quick flash of short skirt.

Bartlett glanced down and away. "Let's talk in a private room." He gestured toward the hallway.

"I wish I could, but I need to get back to Dallas. But I wanted to come by in person to ask if we could meet up over coffee. Could you come to the city? The Dark Brew is usually empty around eleven, after the Sunday morning rush. Do you know where it is?"

"I can find it," he answered with a curt nod.

"Thank you." Janet gave the young officer a little flutter of dark lashes. "I really appreciate it."

Bartlett shifted from one foot to the other, then motioned for Janet to step a bit further away from the desk. "Anyone else involved in this wild ride you had?"

"You met my friend, Molly. She had to come rescue me. It involves Ray Boyd and some of his hired help. I'm worried that they're trying to track down Merilee's car at the impound here. I think she's got incriminating information and doesn't even know it. None of us are feeling too safe right now."

Bartlett stroked his chin as he studied her face, then glanced over his shoulder to check that the other officer wasn't listening. "I oversee the impound lot, and it's secure. I'll tell you that things don't look great for Merilee at this point, so if you have any information to share that could help in this investigation, great." Reaching for the doorknob, he waved her out. "I'll see you at eleven, Janet."

Janet scooted down the station's concrete stairs and headed toward her bug. *Thank goodness he took the meeting*, she thought. *Let's hope Molly got her brother onboard.*

Chapter 9 *(by Mary Koppel)*

As predicted, the Dark Brew—an artsy, funky coffee shop in the girls' neighborhood—was almost empty when they arrived there a few hours later. The usual Sunday morning crowd had moved on, so there were plenty of open tables. Janet went to order drinks while Molly got a table close to the door. She settled into her chair and checked her phone. Denzel had agreed to meet with them, but Molly had detected a slight note of something in his voice. Reluctance? Surely not. Denzel had said he wanted to help get Merilee out of this mess.

"Oh, it's you."

Molly looked up at Officer Bartlett and pressed her lips together, unsure how she should respond.

Bartlett immediately turned scarlet. "I mean, oh my gosh, I didn't mean it that way. I just thought . . ." He unconsciously scratched his arm.

"You just thought what?" Molly prompted. She blinked at him, turning over her phone and placing it on the table to give him her full attention.

He sucked in a breath and deflated, "I thought I was meeting with just Janet. I'm sorry. I was rude. May I sit down?"

Pleasantly surprised by Bartlett's manners—which had been quite different when they'd met at the station, and even when he'd pulled her over—Molly silently motioned at the chair across from her.

"You thought she was asking you out?" Molly offered, resting her chin on her fist and feeling a twinge of sympathy for Bartlett.

"I hoped so, but I guess not." He looked hopefully at Molly and she shook her head. He slumped into the chair and placed the folder he was carrying on the table.

"Is that the case against Merilee?" Molly changed the subject and went to reach for the folder. Bartlett slapped a large hand down on it. She snatched her hand back and looked at him.

"Yes, it is, but I don't think that you and Janet are going to want to see this."

Molly raised her eyebrows. Bartlett didn't sound angry or defensive. He actually sounded a little sad, which caught Molly off guard.

In a bustle of energy, Janet hurried up to the table and set the drinks down, interrupting Molly's thoughts. "Molly, here's your tea. I have Denzel's granita and my soy latte. Officer Bartlett, what would you like?"

"It's Eric. Call me Eric," he said. Then he sighed and shook his head. "Who's Denzel?" He looked back and forth between Molly and Janet.

"That would be Detective Jones." Denzel stood behind Bartlett's chair with his arms crossed. Molly smiled up at her older brother. He looked sharp in his blue blazer and tie. He must have come straight over from church.

Bartlett twisted around and stood up abruptly, almost sending his chair flying behind him. Luckily, Denzel caught the chair and righted it. Bartlett nervously introduced himself and the two men shook hands. Janet stood and hugged Denzel as he made his way around the table to take a seat next to Molly.

"Okay, what did I miss?" He lifted his granita and sipped it though the straw. His eyes did not leave Bartlett's as he sized up the lanky officer across from him.

"Uh, well, I've been investigating my Aunt June's—
I mean June Mason's death." Bartlett took a breath,
"The whole case did not sit right with me. I'm a
relative, so I wasn't on the team that investigated at the
scene. But in my opinion, something's off. And reports
were missing." He looked at the others at the table.
"Truth is, I didn't have the privilege of knowing my
aunt, and that's another story. But from everything I've
heard about her, including from Merilee, June was not a
clumsy woman."

"Because she wasn't clumsy, she couldn't have had
an accident?" Denzel's stare was laser focused.

Molly and Janet sat silently and watched the two
men.

"I get that. But I looked at the preliminary medical
report—once I finally found it. Seems it had gotten lost
in the shuffle around the Shotgun City PD. Anyway, it
looks like June sustained a head injury—but not the
kind you'd get in a fall. More like the kind that comes
from being struck on the head. From behind. It just
didn't add up, so I picked up the investigation and
requested the ME review the case. Well, he did this
week, and concluded that we're dealing with a
homicide—not an accident."

Janet leaned back from the table and rubbed her
arms, as if trying to rub away the image of lively June
Mason being murdered. She shook her head. "But that
doesn't mean Merilee did it. We know her. She'd never
do something like that!"

Molly watched Bartlett's demeanor change when
Janet said Merilee's name. She also noticed that
Denzel's gaze dropped to the tabletop.

"How well do you really know Merilee?" Bartlett
asked Janet.

"What do you mean? I've known her since we were
kids. So has Molly. We all live in the same building

now—just around the corner from here. I'd say we know her pretty darn well."

Molly nodded in agreement.

"I mean, when was the last time you actually spent a lot of time with her. You know, like, quality time? When was the last time you all had coffee? Did you know what was going on with her?" Bartlett leaned closer on this last sentence.

"What are you saying?" Molly asked. "We see her a lot. Maybe not as much since we finished school, because we all have our own lives—you know. We go to work, we have different schedules, different habits. But we're around each other a lot." Molly could feel her face getting warmer.

Again, Denzel looked uncomfortable. He shifted in his chair. Molly knew her brother—and she could tell he knew something he was hesitating to share.

"Do you know where she works? Do you know what she does with her free time?" Bartlett went on.

"Of course. She used to spend a lot of time helping at the ranch. Now she works at a call center. What does this have to do with anything?" Molly looked at her brother again, waiting for him to chime in about Merilee, but he was silent.

Bartlett shook his head. Denzel raised his hand, as if trying to signal for Bartlett to stop talking, but he went on, "Merilee hasn't worked full time for at least a year . . ."

"But . . ." Janet interrupted. Her mouth opened and then shut.

Molly slumped back in her chair, shocked.

Bartlett continued: "Merilee's had some trouble with drug use over the past five years."

Janet started to protest, but Bartlett held up a hand. "Now hear me out," he said. "When she was pulled over Friday night when you two were speeding out of Shotgun City, a test was run because of the crazy way Merilee was acting. And I'm sorry to say that a few different drugs were found in her system. Thing is, it didn't look good, because of the past and because she had a couple of outstanding tickets."

"But that's because Merilee is . . . well, Merilee. She forgets things like parking tickets, but remembers things like the capitols of every state or the words to every song she ever heard. That's how she is," said Janet.

Bartlett looked at Denzel.

"What?" Molly asked incredulously. "Denzel, you know something you're not telling us. Out with it!"

Denzel looked at his sister with serious eyes. "When Merilee got into trouble, June was desperate to help her."

"And?"

"About a week before June's death, Merilee was overheard fighting with her."

"Someone actually called the station," Bartlett added. "I wasn't there at the time, but an officer went out to the Flying B to check on things."

"Well, I wonder who called to complain," said Janet angrily. "Hmm. Maybe old Highway Ray? I'd bet anything—"

"The caller didn't identify himself. But when the police came out to the ranch, they made Merilee leave. Apparently, June explained that she'd just told Merilee that she had cut her off financially until she straightened out. And Merilee got angry." Bartlett leaned back in his chair.

"But it was probably that jerk Officer Scott or one of his buddies who reported all that!" said Molly. "I could tell that guy was crooked. How do we really even know for sure that's the truth?"

Janet wiped her eyes with the back of her hand and sniffled. "Merilee had always been so close to June," she said. "This cannot be the truth. Can't you see Merilee is being framed? And now she's in jail and who's going to believe her side of the story?"

Molly patted her friend on the shoulder. This meeting had certainly taken an unexpected turn. "But think about it. Why wait? If Merilee had flown into a murderous rage, wouldn't she have killed June right there on the spot? I mean, isn't that how crimes of passion work? And if Merilee was already cut off financially, she wouldn't have benefitted in any way from her mother's death. So what was her motive?" Molly turned the facts over and over in her mind. "And why did those guys—Raymond Boyd and that Jax guy—basically kidnap Janet if this whole business with Merilee going to Shotgun City to see her uncle doesn't have something to do with June's death? What do they want?"

Janet and Molly proceeded to tell Bartlett and Denny every detail of the night before—about going to Guitars and Cadillacs; about Jax tricking Janet; about Justine and Molly going after them.

"So you think June's death is suspicious. So do we," Janet said to Bartlett. "And Merilee clearly has a few strikes against her—real or fabricated."

Bartlett and Denny both nodded.

"We have to get at the truth," said Molly. "Because Ray Boyd is up to no good, and whatever those reports say, you've got the wrong person behind bars."

The four around the table were silent for a moment. Bartlett looked down at his wristwatch and back at the group. "I'm sorry. I've got to go."

"So do I," said Denny apologetically.

"You two stay safe," said Bartlett, looking at Molly first, then at Janet. He turned to go, but then stopped and assured the girls that the impound lot was heavily guarded, and that he'd try to get into the car as soon as it was safe. "Please. Leave the investigating to the police," he added, and with a nod, turned and left the coffee shop.

"He's right about that, sis," said Denny, giving Molly a kiss on the top of her head. "Lay low until we get to the bottom of this." With one last backward glance, he was gone as well.

"*Lay low*," said Molly. "I don't think so." She looked at Janet. "We need to talk to Merilee and get the truth."

Chapter 10 *(by Christina Hazelwood)*

"We've got to do something to help Merilee. This is a mess!" Molly said woefully as she and Janet walked out onto the sidewalk in front of the Dark Brew.

The two walked along in silent contemplation for a moment.

Suddenly, Janet straightened her shoulders. "I think it's time we visited Grandma's."

"What?"

"The only way to help Merilee is to get some kind of concrete evidence, and we need some help for that."

"What does Grandma have to do with it? Hold it: whose grandma are we talking about?" asked Molly.

"There's something in Highway Ray's coat. We've got to get into Merilee's ugly green Kia and find out what it is. There's only one guy I can think of who might be able to help us, and that's Duncan—and he lives—"

"At his grandma's," Molly and Janet said simultaneously.

"But Bartlett said he'd go look when it's safe. Shouldn't we just wait for him to report back?" asked Molly.

"We've known Bartlett for, what? Two days? Are we a hundred percent sure of him? I just don't want to risk losing whatever it is Ray left in his jacket. Merilee's freedom—and maybe even the key to this entire mess—is in the back of that car."

Molly frowned, worried. "But Bartlett said the place was 'heavily guarded.'"

"Think about it, Molly. We're talking about the Shotgun City impound. I mean, there are like five officers in the whole department."

"I have a feeling I'm going to regret this," said Molly as the two friends piled into the Civic and headed out of the city, through the countryside and right back to the old Victorian house owned by Huey Duncan's Tupperware-selling grandmother.

"You think he'll help us?" Molly asked.

"The number of tattoos he's got plus the fact that he throws parties while his grandmother's out of town indicate that Duncan is a risk-taker," Janet said, holding up crossed fingers.

They parked the Civic in a spot where they could watch the front door without being obvious, then played Rock-Paper-Scissors to decide which of them would approach first. Molly, the scissor loser, slumped up to the door, turned for a quick look back at Janet who was waiting in the stakeout car, and rang the doorbell. After a few rings and no answer, Molly gave up and retreated to the car.

"Now what do we do?" she asked, pulling at the scrunchie on her wrist.

"We wait," said Janet.

"Duncan may not show up for hours!"

"Yeah, well Merilee's in jail," said Janet. "I think we can tough it out."

Two hours later, Duncan arrived home, fumbling with his keys and juggling loaded grocery bags. Janet and Molly jumped out of the Civic and rushed at Duncan just as he was closing the door.

"Hi, Duncan! Remember us?" Molly said cheerfully.

Startled, Duncan said, "Duh. I just saw you yesterday. You're the ones with the flat tires from the party."

"That's right," Janet said. "And you're the guy whose dad has the only towing service in town."

"We wonder if you could help us out," Molly said. "Merilee, our friend who was at your party, got her Kia Soul impounded over at the police department, and there's something in her car we need."

Duncan looked back and forth at their pleading faces. "You want me to help you get something out of police lock-up?"

Molly nodded.

Janet said, "Yep."

When Duncan looked at them like they were crazy, Janet said, "Merilee's life depends on it. We just need to see what's in the back seat of her car."

"Your dad tows cars into the police lot all the time, right? You must know how to get in there," Molly said. "We won't hurt anything. We just need to check Merilee's car and then we'll be on our way. We even have her spare key."

"It's the only way we can help her," Janet added, looking as pitiful as she knew how.

Duncan contemplated this. "I could probably figure something out," he said slowly. "But what's in it for me?"

"We would both be very grateful," said Janet, flashing her blue eyes and smiling. Duncan gave Janet a dubious look.

"I could throw in some of my mom's famous home cooking," Molly offered.

That did the trick. "Well, this is a slow night, so I could probably . . ." Duncan's voice trailed off. Then he looked sternly at each of them. "You'll have to do exactly as I say!"

"We will," Molly assured him, as Janet nodded.

"Okay. Meet me at my dad's shop at two a.m. Wear dark clothes and bring flashlights. And, of course, not a word to anyone."

"Absolutely!" said Molly.

"Thanks, Duncan," said Janet. "We'll go home and get a little rest, then head back here tonight. See you in a few hours."

Chapter 11 *(by Rosie Pease)*

"Are you seriously wearing that tonight?" Janet asked Molly upon entering her friend's bedroom.

Molly, who'd been tying her black running shoes, looked up at the mirror, at her form-fitting outfit: black yoga pants and a snug but comfortable black long-sleeved t-shirt. "Of course I am," she said, her eyes shifting to Janet's reflection.

"You look like a cat burglar."

"Thanks. That's what I was going for." Molly pulled her box braids behind her head and tied them back with her scrunchie. "If we're breaking into a place, we might as well look the part. The question is, why are you wearing *those*?" She pointed at Janet's shoes.

Janet lifted a foot to inspect her thick-soled combat boots. "Duncan said to wear dark clothing. These are the only black shoes I have besides a pair of pumps." She'd tucked her dark jeggings into the boots and was wearing a navy sweatshirt over a dark gray t-shirt.

"But you'll never be able to run away in those if we get caught. You really ought to invest in a decent pair of tennis shoes."

"Well, that's the thing," Janet said with a smile. "I don't intend to get caught. You ready to go?"

Molly pulled the bow of her laces tight, then stood. "I am now. Let's go meet Duncan."

The two climbed into Molly's Civic and took off for Shotgun City and Duncan's father's garage.

"I can't stop wondering what Ray could have in Merilee's car that he wants so badly," Janet said after failing to find anything good to listen to on the radio.

"I know. I sure hope whatever it is can help poor Merilee." Molly paused and looked at Janet. "You don't believe what they're saying about her, do you?"

"Nope. There's no way she killed her mom."

Molly kept her eyes focused on the dark road in front of her. "I *know* that. I'm talking about everything else. Her job, her suspected drug use . . ."

The thought of it all tugged at Janet's heart once more. Surely she wouldn't have missed the signs. They were neighbors, after all. And friends. If Merilee had a serious drug problem, Janet would've picked up on it. And how had Merilee have been paying rent all this time if she didn't have a fulltime job? "I don't know, Moll. Something just doesn't add up."

"Well, once we find out what's in Merilee's car, hopefully we'll start to get answers. And if not, I say we go back to that jail and insist on seeing Merilee. We have to talk to her and get the whole story from her perspective."

"They might not let us go in together when the time comes. And so many things will depend on whether Merilee's been officially charged with her mom's murder yet."

Molly peered at Janet from the corner of her eye and grinned. "I'm sure you can figure something out. Bat your eyelashes at Officer Bartlett so he can pull some strings. He has such a crush on you. He was obviously disappointed when he realized meeting you at the Dark Brew wasn't a date."

Before Janet could think of a response, they crossed into Shotgun City, nearly passing Duncan's tow shop and mechanic garage, hidden along the darkened Church Street.

"This is it," she said. "Quick—turn here and let's park in back."

They pulled around the tow truck that was parked on the side street and into a little employee parking lot next to a beat-up pickup truck with its cabin light on. Huey Duncan lifted his hand in acknowledgement as Molly cut the engine. By the time the two girls were out of the car, flashlights in hand, Duncan was waiting for them behind the truck bed.

"You seem nervous," Molly said, noticing the worried look on Duncan's face. "You're not chickening out, are you?"

"Hey, despite the tattoos, I've never done more than get a little rowdy at a party," Duncan said in his own defense. "Stealing my dad's tow truck to break into a police impound lot for two people I don't know is naturally a little bit nerve-racking, don't you think?" He rubbed the back of his neck.

Both of the girls nodded.

"Fair enough," said Molly.

"I'm gonna need y'all to get in the tow truck and buckle up. It'll only take me a few minutes to hook up your car—"

"Wait, what?" Molly raised an eyebrow at him.

"I told you you'd have to do everything I say. No questions."

"Come on, Moll. We need to do this for Merilee," Janet said, leading Molly to the passenger side of the tow truck. They climbed up onto the front bench seat and waited quietly as Duncan got in and started to back the truck toward Molly's Civic.

When he hopped back out, Molly called, "Be careful!" after him before he could close the door. The Civic might be old and a little out of shape, but it was hers.

A few minutes later, the car was secured onto the flatbed of the tow truck and the three were on their way.

"I figure hooking up your car gives me a reason to be at the impound lot if I'm asked about it," Duncan explained once they were on the road. "But I'm gonna unload it right before we enter the lot, just in case you need a getaway car. I don't know what you're after, and I don't *want* to know, but if you say it could mean life or death for your friend, I figure you might need to be able to make a quick escape. Especially seeing as who she was fighting with at Grandma's."

Molly didn't know whether to be impressed by Duncan's plans or worried that he'd incorporated an escape scheme into them—and that he might be right about them needing to hightail it out of the impound. "What do you know about those guys Merilee was arguing with?" she asked. "I thought you said you didn't even get home from work until three a.m. and then fell asleep on the couch the night of the party."

"Well . . ." Duncan hedged. "Shotgun's a small town. I might've heard something about it. I really only know Gibbs. He's a foreman at the Flying B. But those ranch hand guys seem like a rough bunch. Things like that fight with your friend? That kind of thing follows those guys around. There was a big bunch of them at the party at Grandma's that night. I recognized most of them, but there were a couple of new guys."

Molly leaned close to Janet and whispered, "Wonder if our friend Jax was one of the new guys."

Janet nodded. "Or Officer Scott, from the police station. I'm positive he was one of the guys Merilee argued with."

"I'm sitting right here, you know," said Duncan, rolling his eyes. "I can hear you two whispering."

Neither Janet nor Molly quite knew how to respond. Duncan seemed, contrary to their first impression of him, to be a pretty trustworthy guy. But as he himself had said, Shotgun was a very small town. For all they knew, Duncan might've gone way back with any of those guys—and they certainly weren't at liberty to tell him that Bartlett was Merilee's cousin and was looking into his aunt's murder. Or that Janet had been kidnapped by Jax the night before.

Eventually, Janet said, "We're just trying to figure out what's going on with our friend and how the guys she was arguing with might be involved."

Duncan nodded but said nothing more. He'd told them all he knew.

Within a few minutes, they were pulling up at the impound lot, which was dark and quiet.

Janet wondered who was guarding it and how. "This place looks pretty secure," she said, turning to Duncan. "Any idea what the security situation is here?"

"Yep," said Duncan, getting out of the tow truck. He unloaded Molly's Civic, then appeared in the open window on the passenger side, causing Molly and Janet to jump.

"Here's the deal," he said. "Yes, the place is under guard. But by way of security cameras. I know where the switch is that shuts down the power to the impound. That includes the lights and the cameras. They've had trouble with outages here for years, every time a storm kicks up, so they won't get too riled up when the cameras blink off over at the station." Duncan pointed in the direction of the police station, just around the corner.

"But Duncan, there's no storm right now," said Molly.

There was a sudden rumble of thunder.

"That's why I told you to show up at two in the morning," said Duncan, pointing skyward.

"Duncan! You knew a storm was coming?" said Janet.

"I'm something of an armchair meteorologist," Duncan admitted. "See that giant, honkin' cumulonimbus up there?"

They all looked at the gathering clouds overhead.

"Anyway, after a few minutes, they'll start to wonder why the backup generator isn't kicking on. You're gonna be in the dark and you're gonna have to work fast. I guarantee that red-headed officer will run his patrol car over here, and you'd better be long gone by then."

Janet and Molly looked at each other. "*Bartlett,*" they both said.

"Okay. You ready?" Duncan asked.

Molly gave Janet a small shove toward the door. Duncan opened it for them, and the two slid out and onto the street that ran alongside the impound lot. The lot itself was surrounded by a high chain-link fence, the top of which jutted out toward the street to prevent anyone from being able to climb over it.

"Hope you can run fast if you need to," Duncan said. "It's only been a few days since your friend's car was towed, so I can point you to the general area where it might be. I was here dropping one off a day or two before her car ended up here, so it shouldn't be far from there."

Molly was once again impressed by Duncan's foresight, but Janet glanced down at her own feet with concern, inwardly admitting that maybe Molly had been right about the combat boots.

"I told you," Molly sang quietly. "Good luck running in those."

"Hey. These are a fashion statement."

"Right now, the only statement they're making is, 'We're not designed for running,'" said Molly with a laugh.

When they were near the lot's entrance, Duncan came to an abrupt stop.

"What is it? What's wrong?" asked Janet.

"See that terminal by the gate? With the security keypad?"

"Yes," said Molly.

"Uh, I don't mean to alarm y'all, but we might have company."

"What do you mean?" Janet asked.

"Company like the police?" Molly added, her whisper rising half an octave. She took a steadying breath and reasoned with herself that technically, they hadn't gone inside the lot yet, so they hadn't done anything wrong. If the police approached them right now, they could say they were just out for a stroll . . . at a suspicious place and a very suspicious time.

"No, not the police, but I bet they'll be here soon, too." Duncan pointed at the gate, which stood partway open. "Someone's beat us here. They've busted the terminal and the gate's open. Take my advice. Be quick." Duncan pointed toward the back left-hand corner, deep in the bowels of the impound. "You'll have to go back that way. Get your flashlights ready now. I'm going to flip the switch, and then I'm out of here. You get in and get out. You hear me?"

Both girls nodded nervously.

"I'm off then," said Duncan, starting to jog away.

"Hey Duncan!" Molly called. He stopped and looked back. "Thanks!" she said, giving him a little wave.

Within a few seconds, the lights flipped off, and Molly and Janet switched on their flashlights. "Keep the beams low," whispered Janet. "And keep your head down."

They scurried through the open gate and in the direction that Duncan had pointed them.

"I wonder who broke the gate," said Janet as they moved down the row of cars. "Do you think it could be Ray, or those guys from the ranch? What if they already found what was in Merilee's car?"

"There's no way they've been here long, or the police surely would've already arrived," said Molly.

"Where are you, ugly green Kia Soul?" Janet whispered into the darkness, shining her flashlight this way and that.

"There it is!" Molly's voice came out in an excited whisper. "No way does anyone other than us have that bumper sticker."

They ran semi-crouched toward the Soul with the bumper sticker depicting a flamingo riding a Pegasus. It was special to the three girls—and all three had the same sticker. They always said that Merilee was the Pegasus, because she'd grown up on a ranch, but had always put her own unique spin on things where she could. The flamingo was both Molly and Janet, because one summer, they'd each unknowingly purchased the same pink polka dot bathing suit, and Merilee had teased them, saying they looked like the leggy pink birds.

When they got to the car, Molly and Janet split up, each taking one side to check over.

Janet inspected the passenger side, but found nothing. "Anything on your side, Moll?" she asked.

"There's a coat on the seat!" said Molly, peering into the window.

Janet lifted her flashlight to illuminate the car's interior. "Make that two coats. There's Merilee's, and that other one with it looks like it's from the ranch. I can see part of the Flying B's logo from here."

"Well, that's got to be it, then."

Molly dug into her pocket and produced a key. "Thank you, Merilee, for leaving your spare key with us," she said, inserting the key into the lock and turning it twice. The locks disengaged throughout the car, allowing Molly and Janet to open the back doors.

And set off the Soul's alarm.

"Ahh! I told her to get that fixed months ago," Janet said. "Quick, give me the key!" She reached forward into the driver's seat and jabbed the key into the ignition, praying that starting the car with the key would turn off the alarm.

It did, much to their relief. Janet turned off the car and handed the key back to Molly.

But then a new noise accosted their ears, and it was growing louder by the second.

"Cops! Grab the jacket and let's go!" Janet shouted, jumping out of the car and taking off between two trucks in the next aisle.

Molly grabbed the jackets and clutching them to her chest, took off running toward the exit, but Janet skidded to a halt in the middle of the aisle between two rows of cars.

"What are you doing? Let's go!" Molly yelled.

Janet waved her friend off. "Go! I left the door open on Merilee's car! I'm going back so it won't look like we've been here."

"Don't be ridiculous!" said Molly. "We have to get out of here. Now!"

"Bartlett will know it was us!" said Janet. "I'm going back!"

"Fine. I'll get the car started. Meet you there!" Molly yelled, and she disappeared into the darkness. A loud clap of thunder sounded overhead and outside, the rain started falling in earnest.

Janet sped back to Merilee's Kia and slammed the back door shut, then ducked into a shadow just as police headlights illuminated the open area by Merilee's car. Janet breathed a sigh of relief that Molly had gotten away—but the relief was short-lived as fear flooded in that she wouldn't be as lucky.

The moment the police car slowly moved on, Janet scrambled to get away—but she went the opposite direction from the way Molly had gone. She'd have to take the long way around. Janet once again cursed her choice of footwear.

Chapter 12 *(by Shawn Shallow)*

Back at the ranch, Ray decided to check on the boys. Awakened by a clap of thunder, he'd noticed the lights still on over at the bunkhouse. He'd checked the clock. Yep, his toadies at the police department should be at the impound lot this very minute, collecting his jacket. It had been tricky— first, paying them enough to get them to take the risk. And then, figuring out how to get around the troublesome Officer Bartlett. If only he could've bought off Bartlett, things would've so easy. He never would've had to bother with kidnapping the beautiful but stubborn Janet. And he sure wouldn't have had to trust the idiots he'd sent over to the impound tonight.

Thunder rolled overhead as Ray flung open the bunkhouse door—with a bang for maximum effect. The boys withdrew in a hurry from where they'd been standing, surrounding Jax, who was holding a find of great interest. Ray kicked aside a beer can as he walked over to take a closer look. On its own, the wild west relic would make a statement in anyone's collection and fetch a modest sum at auction. But Ray knew in an instant—at a glance—that this particular relic was the key to something much more.

He made sure to keep his voice calm and steady as he snatched the old gun belt. "Where'd you find this?" he asked.

"Around Packsaddle Mountain, where you had us digging posts. It ain't worth anything. Look at the hole," said Jax, defensively pointing at the ripped leather in the old cartridge loop.

Packsaddle Mountain—ironically classified as a "mountain" because it was the biggest hill in a county that was mostly plains—took up the western boundary of the Flying B.

Folding the gun belt and tucking it under his arm, Ray couldn't believe this windfall. *Lucky for me that boy don't know enough to drink upstream from the herd, let alone know what he's found*, he thought.

"Give it back. It's mine. I found it," exclaimed Jax, grabbing at the belt.

The other ranch hands watched for a frozen second to see if Ray would let that remark slide, or if his temper would take over, as it often did. Sure enough, Ray's temper won. In a flash, Jax was on the ground with a bloody nose. The "fight" was over before it had begun.

"Next time, remember who owns this land, and everything on it," Ray growled as he pushed through the little group and stomped out of the bunkhouse, trying to appear enraged—all the while, inwardly smiling ear-to-ear. He ran his thumb over the small letters that had been burned into the leather: *SB*. This old gun belt had very likely belonged to Sam Bass—an outlaw who'd been known to frequent the area back in the day—and it was the very thing that justified the crap show Ray had unleashed on his sister, now dead, and her daughter, now framed for murder.

As he hurried across the yard through the rain toward the big house, Ray reflected on how it had all started with a simple card game just six months earlier. The ranch hands were playing poker and going heavy on the whiskey, as usual. What *wasn't* usual was the makeshift poker chips they were playing for. Mixed in with the dinged plastic chips and quarters were a handful of tarnished coins that caught Ray's attention. He'd grabbed one and examined it closely.

"Where'd you get these?" he'd asked, looking at the boys.

"Found 'em out in the foothills around Packsaddle—where we're putting in the new fence."

The boys thought they were playing with old, beat-up quarters. But despite being black with tarnish, Ray had instantly identified the 1875 Liberty Head. Fortunately, those knot heads hadn't enough sense to rub off the tarnish to reveal the gold underneath.

To Ray—who'd admired and made a study of the outlaws who used to haunt this area—the coins supported a theory he'd had for a long, long time: that somewhere in the hills of the Flying B lay Sam Bass's old hideout. Locals had looked for it for over a century—and it was right under Ray Boyd's nose. And if the stories were true, Bass had left behind a fortune, lost to history and legend—until now.

Ray smiled as he thought back to how he'd quickly settled his own racing pulse and hidden his glee at finding such a treasure on the poker table. "You boys been working too hard. The least I can do is get you some decent poker chips from the house and a stake to play with."

The hands had looked at each other in shock. *Was this the Highway Ray they'd come to know and hate?*

After returning from the house, Ray had casually scooped up the old coins and replaced them with a sawbuck for each player—and even though the boys had to suspect that something was up, no one wanted to look a gift horse in the mouth, much less snap Ray out of his rare benevolent mood.

The boys never caught on, even though most everyone in town knew that somewhere, local boy Sam Bass had an old hideout containing loot from his robberies that had never been recovered. As the story went, Bass and his gang had hightailed it back to Texas after their biggest haul—the robbery of a train carrying newly minted Liberty Head twenty-dollar gold pieces from the San Francisco mint to Big Spring Station, Nebraska.

Bass had forced the station master to halt the gold-laden train. Once onboard, Bass's men had no trouble opening the simple "way safe," but found only a handful of cash inside. Dissatisfied with the meager take, Bass had pulled a gun on the hapless conductor and forced him to open the impregnable "through safe," protected by a time lock set to open only once the train had reached its destination.

And that was how they'd hit the mother lode: sixty thousand dollars' worth of the gold pieces, still warm from the San Francisco Mint. The gang divided the coins between themselves and made their escape in different directions. Only Bass and his buddy Jack David managed to evade capture with the lion's share of the take—worth about 340 million in today's dollars.

Bass used to brag that his only scratch from these events was a hole in his gun belt from flying posse bullets. The very hole Ray was looking at right now as he marveled at the gun belt Jax had found.

He ran up the porch steps and went inside the ranch house, shaking off the rain and leaving the lights off as he walked back to the master bedroom. Prior to finding those gold coins, he'd tried as hard as he could to get his sister to depend on him at the ranch. After all, she needed help after her husband had died. What a stroke of luck *that* had been. And besides, it wasn't really fair that their parents had left the place entirely to June.

They always did like her best. But the appearance of those coins that day meant Ray had to do whatever was necessary to make the ranch his. One day, it had come to him—a simple yet brilliant plan. All he had to do was substitute a fake will with himself as the beneficiary.

And get rid of June.

He flicked on his bedside lamp and retrieved an old trunk containing the loose coins along with old newspaper clippings he'd gotten from the library. In a strange way, Ray identified with Bass and enjoyed the research. Bass had no morals, no manners, no God. Killing a person, even a sister, came as natural as shooting an animal. It was a simple matter of survival of the fittest, wasn't it?

Ray carefully placed the gun belt into the trunk and went to mark where Jax had found it on his map. But the map wasn't there. Ray rifled through the trunk and then sat back in a cold sweat. Nobody knew this trunk was here. And nobody but him should see that map! He stood and paced for a minute to clear his mind. Then he recalled putting the map into the inside pocket of his jacket when he'd gone out to search the trail last week.

The irony of the situation struck him like a punch to the gut. It was the same jacket he'd worn when he'd gone to the bank with Merilee on Friday. So now, both June's original will and the map with all of Ray's notes about Bass's hideout were in June's daughter's car. If anyone found them, he'd be ruined.

But all of that was under control now. Ray took a deep breath. Merilee was in jail. And really, it was a good thing her car had been impounded—keeping Ray's jacket locked up safe and sound over the past few days. Soon, he'd have it back.

Ray looked out the front windows of the ranch house, through the pouring rain catching in the moonlight. They should've been here by now. Where were they?

Chapter 13 *(by Zaida Alfaro)*

Janet found it very difficult to tiptoe in her combat boots. It also didn't help that she was not good at directions. She had gotten turned around in the dark, and now had no idea which way it was to where Molly was waiting in the Civic. Janet slowly peeked over a black Toyota Corolla that was missing its passenger-side door. She could still see the police lights flashing blue and red in the distance, but thankfully, the siren was no longer sounding.

"Okay, focus and get out of here," Janet whispered to herself.

Her heart pounded even harder when the lights flickered back on. That meant the security cameras were on, too. Janet could hear the rain pounding, and as another flash of lighting lit the sky outside, she hoped the lights would be knocked out again. She started to semi-crawl in the direction of the exit—or at least she thought she was moving in that direction. When she saw the gate up ahead, she lowered her gaze and quickened her short, squatted steps. She was getting closer to the chain-link fence, when she ran straight into the right shin of a pair of dark blue slacks. She tilted her gaze up, landing on a very irate face.

"What are you doing here at three in the morning?" Officer Bartlett said in a shocked whisper.

Janet slowly stood up, subtly looking toward the exit for Molly or their car—not wanting Bartlett to spot Molly as well. "Oh, I was just . . . you know, I was in town and I was, um, looking for Merilee's car," she replied, thinking that maybe it would be a good idea to tell the truth, and hoping that Bartlett really and truly wanted to help Merilee.

Bartlett stood motionless, waiting for a more detailed response, and Janet felt beads of sweat popping out on her forehead.

"Please tell me you're not the person who tripped the breaker," he finally said.

"I did not trip the breaker," Janet pledged.

"We already discussed this. Do you have any idea what kind of trouble we could get into if we tamper with that car? There are eyes everywhere." Bartlett glanced up, and Janet saw the security camera looking down at them. Bartlett gave her a tight glare. "Do you know how lucky you are that it's just me who responded to the alarm?" he said through clenched teeth. He cleared his throat and raised his voice, sounding official as he said, "I'll ask you again: what are you doing here?"

"Well, I was—"

"I'm sorry, miss, that's not good enough." Bartlett now sounded like he was talking to a complete stranger—or a criminal. "I have no choice but to take you to the station."

"For what?" Janet whispered loudly.

"For breaking and entering police property," Bartlett whispered back.

"I didn't break. I only entered. The gate was open."

"Where's Molly?" Bartlett whispered.

"She didn't come with me. She's not involved. I'm here on my own."

Bartlett gave her the *Yeah, right* expression. "How did you get here?" he asked.

Janet slightly shifted her body to the right, and placed her hand on her hip, "I called a Lyft."

"Let's go," Bartlett said, back to his all-business voice.

"Where?" Janet asked as she followed him to his squad car.

"To the station."

"But—"

"I don't want to hear it. Get in." Bartlett opened the back passenger-side door, and Janet got in. Bartlett turned the flashing lights off, and drove out of the lot toward the station nearby. "I need you and Molly to let me do my job from here on in. Do you understand how dangerous this situation is?"

"Well—"

"I get it. You want to help Merilee. So do I. She's my cousin. She's family—and pretty much all the family I have. If I'm honest, I don't think she had anything to do with her mother's death. But if you and Molly keep getting in the way, I can't keep my focus where it needs to be. I can't help her." Janet heard a hint of what sounded like compassion in Bartlett's voice.

"I understand." Janet looked glumly out the window, noticing that the stars were shining brightly, as if they didn't understand how screwed up things were. She felt hopeless, wanting so badly to help her friend, and feeling oddly comforted that she shared that sentiment with Bartlett. "I just wish I could do something," she said. "Merilee isn't perfect. But she's always been there for me."

They pulled into the police station. Bartlett parked the car and swiveled to look back at Janet, a slight smile on his face.

"I just know I'm going to regret this," he said with a sigh. "I'm taking you to jail."

"To jail? You're taking me to jail?" Janet felt the panic rising.

"I'm placing you in a holding cell, so you can think about what you've done."

"But I didn't do anything so wrong, did I?" Janet was close to crying, her heart pounding. She'd never been arrested, let alone put in jail. Would her record be tarnished? Would she lose her job and be known as a criminal? "I—"

"I'm putting you in a holding cell, next to Merilee."

"But—wait what?" Janet asked.

"Are you ready?" Bartlett grinned once again.

Janet took a deep breath, finally realizing what Bartlett was up to. "Ready," she said.

At this hour, the police station was desolate. Bartlett quickly escorted Janet through the station, told the only officer they saw that Janet had been drinking, lowering his voice and saying, "Just want to teach her a lesson," and giving the other officer a wink. He nodded and waved them through, tossing Bartlett the keys. Bartlett hurriedly led Janet to the holding cell right next to Merilee, as promised.

"Now. You have an hour," he whispered to Janet.

"Understood."

Now alone in the holding cell, Janet looked to her right, and saw a figure laying on a twin-sized metal bed, facing the cement wall.

"Merilee."

The person stirred.

"Merilee," Janet called to her again, a little bit louder.

"Janet?" Merilee rolled over and faced Janet. "Oh my gosh!" She jumped up from the bed and ran to the cell bars, reaching through them to hold Janet's hands.

"I didn't do it, Janet. I would never hurt my mom. You have to believe me." Merilee's voice was hoarse, as though she'd been trying to prove her innocence for hours.

Janet's heart broke. "I know you didn't. That's why I'm here. But I don't have much time. Only an hour."

Merilee looked at Janet's combat boots, then back at her face. "You're wearing your cute date-night boots?"

"It's a long story."

They both smiled and sat down on the floor, facing each other, only the cell bars between them.

"Thank you for believing me," Merilee said softly.

"I know you. And, so does Molly. We're both trying to solve this thing. Like—like in those old episodes of *Charlie's Angels*."

Merilee smiled. "I love that show," she said with a sniffle.

"I'm ready to listen." Janet said. "Tell me what happened."

"I've been set up—not only with my mother's murder, but the drug and alcohol use. Janet, I was drugged on Friday—Uncle Ray gave me something and took me to the bank, to Mom's safe deposit box. When they arrested me that night, the cops said they'd found a suspicious baggie in my pocket. But Janet, I swear it wasn't mine. And now, Ray would do anything to keep me from telling the truth." Merilee looked down at her hands. "I'm scared."

"The truth about what?" Janet leaned forward and put her hand on the bars between them.

"Mom, Ray, the ranch, and the millions of dollars at stake."

Chapter 14 *(by Diane Weiner)*

Janet shivered in the dampness of the jail cell. The only sounds were the death-knell rattle coming from the rusty air conditioning unit perched high up in the window, and the drip, drip, drip of the resulting water condensation, which formed dark streaks and culminated in a small puddle on the floor next to Merilee's rusty cot. Janet wanted to talk to her friend about so many things, but she knew their time was limited.

"Go on, tell me. We've only got an hour."

"Mom didn't leave me out in the cold, and I certainly didn't kill her. Ray's framing me."

Janet let out a long sigh. "I knew it. That man is pure evil."

"I think he killed Mom. In fact, I'm sure he did. I've gone over and over this in my mind—and it hasn't been easy, because I was so out of it Friday." Merilee sighed. "Seems like a million years ago. I can't believe it's only been—what day is this?"

"Technically it's Monday, but it's well before sunrise," said Janet. "So go back to Friday. Tell me what happened."

"Janet, I can't even remember most of that evening," said Merilee. "I do remember when I got the message to come to Shotgun. Justine and I were getting ice cream Friday afternoon, and this text came from Uncle Ray. I hadn't talked to him for months, but his message said there was an emergency at the ranch. He begged me to come. Said it wouldn't take long."

Merilee put a hand to her forehead and closed her eyes. "I knew Duncan was having a party that night, and thought it'd be fun. I even invited Justine to come along. She said the Flying B gave her the creeps—probably because an ex-boyfriend of hers works there now. So I dropped her at Vern's—the coffee shop on the square. And then I went out to meet Ray at the ranch. He had a pitcher of lemonade, and poured us both a glass. I remember I was thirsty, and took a big swig of it. And that's when things get blurry in my memory. Janet, I think Ray slipped something into the lemonade."

Janet felt rage rising in her throat. "Well, that explains why you were so weird when I came to pick you up at that party."

"I have this hazy recollection of waking up in Ray's truck, then going into the bank with him. They asked me for my ID . . . I vaguely remember wondering why. And then we were in the safe, where the safe deposit boxes are. I sat down and . . . It's so hazy."

"I know it's hard, but try to remember," said Janet.

"This is going to sound crazy, but I could swear Ray tucked something into his jacket pocket from my mother's safe deposit box."

Janet felt her heart pound, knowing that this was the same Jacket Molly now had—and knowing it must contain the key to everything . . . But also that having it in their possession put them in serious danger.

"Do you think Ray stole something from your mom? Is that what he was doing?"

"But why would he do that? He'd already inherited her entire estate. What else is there to steal? I don't get it." Merilee shook her head, at a loss.

"What did your mother keep in the safe deposit box?"

"I don't know. A bunch of papers. Some old pictures. I should've come over to Shotgun and gone through it all after Mom died, but I just haven't been able to bring myself to do it. I remember Uncle Ray saying he needed to get something out of it, and he needed my signature at the bank to get into it." Merilee groaned. "I never should've trusted him, and I wouldn't have trusted him. But once he drugged me, I was just a pawn. If only I hadn't drunk that lemonade . . ."

"There's no way you could've seen any of this coming," said Janet, laying a reassuring hand over Merilee's.

"I remember when Ray mentioned the safe deposit box in the first place. I remember thinking it was time I had a look at Mom's papers anyway. But then, everything went foggy, and the next thing I remember, I was back at the ranch. It was so strange. I was furious, but I don't know why. I was yelling at Ray about something, and he just sat there, smiling like the cat that ate the canary. I remember grabbing my coat and storming out—and then I was driving back to Vern's to pick up Justine and go to the party at Duncan's."

"That Duncan is a piece of work." Janet smiled at the memory of their tattooed helper.

"Everyone in Shotgun knows the Duncans," said Merilee. "They're a little rough around the edges, but they're good people. And I guess you met my cousin, too." Merilee pointed in the direction of the closed door that led into the station office.

"Bartlett? Yeah, you're going to have to tell Molly and me all about him after we get you out of this mess. You have a cousin we didn't even know about!"

"I know—and I'll tell you all about it when there's time. Kind of a long story."

Janet lowered her voice to a whisper. "Is he trustworthy?"

"I'm not sure yet," said Merilee. "I truly hope so." She paused and shook her head. "I still can't believe my mother left me nothing in her will. I mean, we had our issues, but not even a measly piece of jewelry to remember her by? It doesn't make sense."

Janet, who was beginning to think her shivering had nothing to do with the temperature, but was more about her uneasiness at being locked in a jail cell, hugged herself. "Merilee, why didn't you tell Molly and me you'd lost your job?"

"I . . . I was too embarrassed. I— how can I say this?" Merilee lowered her eyes.

"Seriously? It's me you're talking to. We tell each other everything."

Merilee slowly raised her eyes, forcing herself to look at her friend. "I . . . I got . . ." She cleared her throat. "Remember when I fell off the horse at the ranch? Back before Mom died?"

"Yes, of course. You're lucky there wasn't permanent damage. You were in the hospital for weeks. Your mom was beside herself."

"It was pretty bad." Merilee nodded. "The doctor prescribed Oxy for the pain and it worked too well. I wound up getting hooked and I just couldn't pull myself out of it."

Janet scooted a bit closer to the bars and squeezed Merilee's hand. "You could have come to Molly and me."

"I should have. I know that now. But I thought I could handle it, and like I said, I was embarrassed. Ashamed is a better word. And Janet, it gets worse. I took money from my mother to buy pills after I ran out of refills, and when she figured it out, she cut me off financially. Said she would reinstate my allowance once I successfully completed rehab." A tear rolled down Merilee's cheek. "She was right, of course. Mom was just acting out of love for me. But I was in a bad place for a while there."

"That explains why someone reported hearing yelling coming from your mother's house. That must have been when she told you." Janet squeezed Merilee's hand.

"You know, I wonder who might've called in to report that." Merilee couldn't keep the anger out of her voice. She took a deep breath to steady her nerves. "The thing is, I worked really hard at overcoming that addiction. I did go to rehab. Remember when I told you and Molly I was going on that trip for work?"

Janet nodded, the light coming on in her mind. It all made perfect sense now.

"And I *didn't* lose my job. I'd taken a leave of absence to go to rehab. I've been clean for a good while now, and was trying to make a fresh start." Merilee's voice caught in her throat. "But now Mom will never even know, and the cops think I killed her. And thanks to an informant—I'm guessing Uncle Ray again—they know all about my history. Then when they brought me here Friday night, they also found drugs in my system, of course, and that sealed the deal. Who's going to believe a drug addict in court?"

"Not every cop thinks you're a killer," Janet said. "You have a cousin who's trying to help."

"Eric Bartlett," Merilee with a sniff.

"Yep. And get this: He said the toxicology report from your mother's death was missing from the police file. He chased it down and found out she had been drugged when she died."

Merilee drew in a sharp breath, then let it out slowly and shook her head. "You know, it figures. Uncle Ray has someone in the Shotgun City police force under his thumb. I'd bet a million dollars he made good and sure that report got 'lost.' They seem to have some sort of arrangement. I don't trust most of the police in this town as far as I could throw them."

"That explains why Bartlett has been investigating on his own. But, Merilee, he showed us the report. Not only had your mother been drugged, it says she'd suffered a blow to the head. Definitely not consistent with falling off a chair. Bartlett managed to get the report to the medical examiner, and that was enough to reopen June's case. The ME officially ruled her case a homicide this week."

"Which explains why I'm here now." Merilee dropped her head into her hands. "Poor Mom. If only I'd been there. Maybe I could've—"

"Merilee, you can't do that. You can't think that way. We have to focus all our effort on getting you out of here. And that means finding the real killer."

"Why drug her *and* hit her over the head?" Merilee asked. "Seems one or the other would have done the trick."

"I have a hunch about that," said Janet. "Maybe Ray drugged her to force her to sign a new will."

Merilee shook her head, looking exhausted and overwhelmed.

"Think about it, Merilee," said Janet. "Ray gets June to sign a new will leaving the ranch to him, then he kills her."

"Uncle Ray has his own money. It's not like he was hurting for cash. Why would he kill to get the Flying B?"

"Maybe there's oil under the ground," said Janet.

A light dawned in Merilee's green eyes. "Or . . ."
She shook her head. "No, never mind. Too far-fetched."

Janet looked at her watch. "Hurry, Merilee. Tell me.
Bartlett will be coming to release me any minute."

"Okay. So, the reason this town is called Shotgun
City is that back in the day, there were supposedly all
kinds of shootouts and outlaws—that kind of thing. The
kind of stuff good Western movies are made of."
Merilee looked at Janet, who nodded. "So, when I was
growing up, Uncle Ray used to tell these stories about a
great train robbery, somewhere up north of Texas.
There was this outlaw, Sam Bass. He supposedly had a
hideout here, some think near our ranch. Anyway,
Bass's loot was never recovered." Merilee smiled
faintly at the memory. "I loved those stories. But the
thing is, I grew up and figured they were just tall tales.
But Uncle Ray . . ." Merilee looked at Janet. "He
believed them."

"Seems like I've heard about Sam Bass somewhere."

"Hey. If you've been to Shotgun City, you've heard
of Sam Bass." Merilee stood and gripped the bars.
"When I was a kid, I even remember a few people
turning up at the ranch, asking questions about whether
we ever searched the property for buried treasure. Of
course, when I heard that, I searched every inch of the
place myself, as best I could anyway."

"I'm guessing you didn't find anything," said Janet,
getting to her feet as well.

"Nope. No way for a kid to cover thousands of
acres." Merilee took a deep breath. "But Janet, what if
Uncle Ray did? Or what if he seriously believes the
money is out there, waiting to be found?"

Somewhere in the shadows, a door creaked. Both
girls looked toward the door leading to the station
office, expecting to see Bartlett. But that remained

closed. Then they heard a slam from the other end of the cell block.

Janet's heart pounded. "Oh my gosh! Do you think someone was listening all this time?"

"If so, it wasn't a prisoner. I'm the only one here. It'd have to be someone who works here."

"Like a cop?"

"Exactly."

They heard the chirp of a buzzer and the station door opened.

Janet looked at Merilee and whispered, "Our time is up. There's Bartlett. Should I tell him about that noise we just heard? Ask him if he knows who was eavesdropping from the other end of the cell block?"

"I . . ."

Bartlett's heavy footsteps grew closer.

"He's on our side. I'm almost sure of it," Janet said quickly.

Bartlett inserted his key into the lock and Janet's cell door creaked open.

"Come on. Your hour is up." He was talking in his official cop voice again, but Janet noticed that on the way out, he winked over his shoulder at Merilee.

Chapter 15 *(by Emma Pivato)*

"I need to talk to you in private, *now*," Janet whispered as she and Bartlett walked through the cell corridor back toward the office. "I have some information to share."

Bartlett stopped and looked down at her. "This morning at ten. Go home and rest a little, then meet me at the Grey Goose Café in Dallas—it's in your neighborhood."

"I know it well," said Janet, nodding. "We go there for waffles on Sundays. It's—"

"Shhh." Bartlett put a hand on Janet's arm. "Listen," he whispered.

They both froze at the sound of steps coming from the office. A moment later, they heard the slam of a door in the distance. Bartlett unlocked the jail wing door and slowly opened it, peeking into the front office and seeing that it was temporarily empty.

"You need to get out of here. Fast," he whispered, holding the door open.

Janet took one final glance back down the row of dingy cells, wishing she could take Merilee by the hand and pull her out of this place.

Janet and Molly arrived at the Grey Goose ten minutes early Monday morning and waited anxiously.

"Can we get three coffees, please?" said Janet, smiling at the waitress as she set glasses of water on the table.

"Look! There he is!" Molly said, and Janet was relieved to see Bartlett walking through the door.

"He won't be thrilled to see me here, you know," Molly added with a smirk. "He does have that Texas-sized crush on you."

"Quiet!" Janet flashed a quick glare at Molly before giving Bartlett a little wave.

He came and sat across from them, and the waitress returned and set steaming cups of coffee, along with sugar and cream in front of them.

"Thanks. I need this," said Bartlett, taking a quick sip of his coffee.

"Late night?" Janet asked, chuckling.

"All in the line of duty, ma'am." Bartlett gave a little salute. "I'll have to make this fast. I'm due back at the station shortly."

"We could've driven over to Shotgun," said Janet. "We've both taken a few days off work this week, to try to focus on helping Merilee."

"You're good friends," Bartlett said, looking back and forth between the two of them. "Merilee's lucky to have you."

"So what was that little wink you gave her last night about?" asked Janet.

"Just letting her know I'm looking out for her," said Bartlett. "I have to be careful about that."

"Why?" asked Molly.

"The other cops," Bartlett said with a little shrug. "This is good ol' boy territory out here, you know. I don't want them to figure out that I'm trying to help my cousin—or that I'm the one stirring up Aunt June's murder investigation."

Janet gave him a small smile. Bartlett was starting to grow on her, and that surprised her. "Merilee thinks a few of those good old boys might just be under Uncle Ray's thumb. What do you think about that?"

"Well, I'd have to agree with her there," said Bartlett.

"Do they happen to have access to drugs?" Molly asked.

"They'd have access to anything we've confiscated if they knew who to ask and could pay the going rate."

"So tell me. How do you fit into the Boyd family?" Janet asked, stirring a generous amount of cream into her coffee. "My understanding is that Ray doesn't have any children and June only had Merilee."

"They had a younger sister. But she died. In childbirth."

"When—"

"When she had me, yes."

"Why has Merilee never talked about you?" Molly asked. "I mean, we've all been close friends since high school."

"She didn't know I existed until after her mother died. And apparently, the loss of her sister was too painful for June to bring up. So for better worse, Merilee never knew about her Aunt Janice. . . Or her cousin. Me."

"Go on . . ." Molly coaxed.

Janet leaned forward and gave Bartlett an encouraging nod.

"My mom—the youngest of the Boyd siblings—was pretty wild when she was seventeen, I guess. When she found out she was pregnant and not even sure who the father was, she ran away to Dallas, to a home for unwed mothers. The people there promised her complete confidentiality and told her they could find good adoptive parents for her child.

"Anyway, during the last months of her pregnancy, she met with several potential families, but the ones she felt would do the best job raising me were an older couple in their mid-fifties, Len and Ella Bartlett. They promised my mother they'd take good care of me, and they did. I grew up in a supportive and loving home."

"How do they feel about you getting involved with your birth mother's family now?" Molly asked.

"They died two years ago, just a few months apart, my father of a heart attack first, and then my mother of stomach cancer."

"I'm so sorry," said Janet, almost reaching across the table to pat Bartlett's hand.

"At Mom's funeral, her best friend handed me an envelope, saying that Mom had left it with her and asked her to give it to me after she was gone."

"What was inside?" asked Molly.

"Everything I just told you. My story."

"So you never knew anything about your birth mother when you were growing up?"

"No. Since she'd died the day I was born, I guess my adoptive parents didn't see much point in telling me about her."

"How did you figure out you're June's nephew—and Merilee's cousin?" Janet asked.

"Mom mentioned my birth mother's name in the letter. Janice Boyd. She said she was from Shotgun City. They'd met several times during the pregnancy."

"So you looked for your family."

"Yep, after a while. I'd always known I'd been adopted, but when my parents died, I . . . I ached to find that I had some family somewhere. *Any* family. My parents didn't have siblings, so I never had cousins or aunts or uncles." Bartlett paused and looked into his coffee cup. "I'd always wondered why my birth mother gave me away. So I decided to look for her relatives."

"Did the Boyds know Janice had had a child? Did they ever come looking for you?" Molly asked.

"No—she'd run away. They searched for her, of course. But when they found out she'd died . . . Well, they didn't know I existed, and Janice was gone. End of story. And the place where I was born had a confidentiality agreement with my birth mother, so they never told the Boyds I existed. I was already safely adopted and gone.

"Anyway, about a year after Mom died, I looked up 'Boyd' in the Shotgun directory and found June's listing. I worked up the courage to call, and Merilee answered."

"Did you get to talk to your aunt?" Janet asked.

"Unfortunately, she'd died just a few weeks earlier. But since I live in Shotgun, it was easy enough for Merilee and me to get together."

"You grew up in Dallas, right? Why move to Shotgun City?" Molly wondered.

"It's just a fluke, really, that I landed in the town where my mother grew up. I graduated from the Police Academy in Dallas four years ago but there were no jobs open there. There was an opening in Shotgun. I applied, and got the job. I've been here just over three years now." Bartlett leaned back in the booth as if telling it all had made him tired.

"Thank you for telling us this," Janet said, and this time, she did reach across and pat Bartlett's hand.

His cheeks reddened a little, and he took another sip of coffee. "So you're a counselor, right, Janet? Is Merilee doing okay? I know the Shotgun jail isn't exactly a four-star hotel."

"She's holding it together. We had a good talk."

"I'm glad. I'm trying to get her out of there, you know. I know she didn't kill June. But I can't prove it yet. And I need to stay on the right side of—"

"The good old boys, right?" Janet nodded in understanding.

"Yep." Bartlett glanced at his watch. "I've got to get back over to Shotgun. What's this information you wanted to share, Janet?"

"There's more than one will." Janet paused as Bartlett absorbed this statement.

"*What?*"

"June Boyd had more than one will," Molly repeated.

"See, we had a hunch that Uncle Ray had a second will—one that he'd either forged or forced June to sign," Janet said. "Merilee confirmed our suspicions when I talked with her last night. She said that she thinks Ray stole something from June's safe deposit box. She saw him stash it in his jacket. She's thought about this a lot, sitting in that cell, but her memory of the day she went to the bank with Ray is sketchy at best."

"Because she was drugged," Bartlett said, nodding.

"Exactly. But what if June's original will—her *actual* will—had stipulated that the ranch be left to Merilee? And what if that will had been safely locked away at the bank?"

"Ray couldn't live with that," said Bartlett. "He'd need to lay his grubby hands on it and destroy it."

"Right. And to do that, he'd have to get into that safe deposit box somehow."

"And he needed Merilee's help to do that," Molly added.

"But if he got hold of the will, he's probably burned it by now," said Bartlett.

"But what if he hasn't gotten hold if it yet?" asked Molly, smiling.

"What are you two getting on about?" Bartlett looked at them, amused.

"Like I said, Merilee remembered Ray putting something into his jacket pocket. And somehow, that jacket ended up in Merilee's car. That's what Molly and I were looking for at the impound lot."

"Ray's jacket?"

"Yes."

Both girls nodded.

"So . . . two wills . . ."

They nodded again.

"And . . . Did you find anything in Merilee's car?"

Molly opened her messenger bag and pulled out the will they'd found in Merilee's Kia, then handed it across the table to Bartlett.

"I know you never knew June, but she was a dear person," Janet said, watching Bartlett unfold the papers. "And she loved her daughter. She would never have left her out of her will. And there's the proof."

Bartlett's eyes widened as he looked over the will. "This is—you two are—I can't believe it."

"Thank you very much," Janet said, grinning. "We are pretty amazing, aren't we?"

"I have to get back over to Shotgun. Listen, I need you to keep this safe." Bartlett passed the will back across the table and Molly put it back into her bag. "It's starting to be clear what Ray was up to. Now, we have to prove that he's a murderer. Before anyone else gets hurt."

Chapter 16 *(by Jenna St. James)*

Janet took another sip of her coffee as Officer Bartlett hurried out the café door. "I noticed you didn't mention anything about the treasure map that was also inside Ray's jacket pocket."

Molly smiled. "You noticed, huh?"

"I don't understand. I thought we decided to trust Bartlett."

"We do trust him," Molly said, "but you also just heard him say Ray has connections with certain members of the Shotgun police force. If I'd shown Bartlett that map . . . I don't know. What if he'd kept it and it somehow fell into the wrong hands? Or what if he trusted the wrong cop, and let that information slip? He's said there are eyes everywhere in Shotgun. We can't risk losing our leverage."

Janet groaned. "Our leverage? What exactly are you saying?"

"I'm saying the map is a huge strike against Ray. It provides plenty of motive for him to want the ranch for himself—and wanting the ranch for himself, well, there's his motive for killing June and forging a will. The map is the key to everything."

"I get that," Janet said, "but explain to me what you mean about us keeping the map for *leverage*?"

Molly grinned. "After we put the will in a safe place, you and I are going to confront—and maybe even capture—a killer."

Janet didn't say anything for a full five seconds. "Are you insane? We can't go out to the ranch and snoop around!"

"I didn't say we were," Molly said. "But you and I both know that by now, Ray has figured out that the will isn't in Merilee's impounded car anymore. And if your old buddy Jax or one of Ray's other henchmen didn't manage to retrieve it, that just leaves us, Janet. You and me."

Janet swallowed. "You really think Ray will know we're the ones who took the jacket?"

"Mark my words: he's going to come for us. I say we meet him head-on."

Janet's mouth dropped open. "Molly, listen to me. We can't do that. That's Bartlett's and your brother's job as policemen, not ours. And speaking of Denny, maybe we should talk to him about this."

"He'll just tell us to go through the proper channels. Wait for the police. We need to act quickly. I mean, how safe do you think Merilee is in a police station where some of the officers are corrupt?"

"But you and I know nothing about—"

"Do you want to see Merilee go to jail for something she didn't do?" Molly demanded. "Or worse, let some *accident* befall her to keep her quiet? If Ray drugged June to get her to sign a fake will, and then killed her, what makes you think he won't drug Merilee and get her to sign a fake murder confession, then kill her too?"

Janet sighed and looked out the window. "You're right."

"So just go with me on this. We have the will—the *actual* will that leaves the Flying B to Merilee instead of Ray. That alone provides motive enough for Ray to have killed June. Bartlett said we'd still have to get proof. So let's bring him the proof. If we can trick Ray into admitting he's the killer by dangling the map in front of his face, we can end this thing. Today."

"And how do you suggest we do that?" Janet asked.

"Let's swing home and stash the will. No—let's hide it at my mom's house. Ray might think to ransack our apartment."

"Oh, for the love of—"

"After that, we'll call Ray, tell him we have the map and we're willing to give it to him if he meets us in a public place to talk."

"One glaring problem," Janet said. "If we have the map, he's going to know we have the will. They were both in the coat pocket."

Molly shrugged. "So I'll lie. I'll say when we snatched the coat, the only thing in it was the map— that if there really was a will, it must have fallen out when we ran through the lot."

"Ray's not going to believe that," Janet argued.

"He'll believe it because it gives him hope," Molly said. "People always believe what they want to believe. He'll think we're just silly little girls who were too dumb to hold onto what we had. I guarantee you, he'll have one of his lackeys go back to the impound and try to find it again."

"Let's say he agrees to meet with us," Janet said. "Then what?"

"We're gonna have our phones set to record, and we're going to tell him we don't care whether or not he killed June—that all we want is Merilee's freedom. We'll tell him he can have the map if he can get her out of jail in Shotgun. We can ask him to make another report go missing or something, like he did before. Ray thinks he's above the system, Janet. I'm fairly certain that if we push the right buttons, he'll end up bragging about how he killed

June. And our job is to act impressed—that'll really get him singing. He's deluded himself into thinking he's invincible and can live outside the law—like some kind of legendary outlaw."

"So we rile him up enough, and his guard goes down, and he says something incriminating?"

"Exactly. We'll simper and flirt and dangle that map and keep him talking until he spills his guts. He'll never think we were clever enough to try and trap him."

Janet closed her eyes and laughed. "I can't believe I'm actually thinking about doing this. It's insane." She opened her eyes. "But okay. Let's do it."

After a quick stop at Molly's mom's house to hide the will and say hello, Janet's little red Bug was once again headed toward Shotgun City.

"What do you suppose is buried at Packsaddle Mountain, anyway?" Molly asked, studying Ray's map. "Coins? Jewelry? Money?"

"Merilee has an interesting theory about that," Janet said, "It has to do with an outlaw and some missing loot that could be worth a fortune. Bottom line: if Ray was willing to kill his own sister for whatever it is, I'm guessing it's pretty significant."

"There are some notes penciled in, but I can't read the chicken scratch."

Janet glanced at Molly. "I seriously hope we're doing the right thing."

As they neared Shotgun City, Molly took out her cell phone. "Okay, I found a number for the Flying B Ranch. We need to decide where we should meet."

"I know," Janet said. "Remember when we went to the police station Saturday? There was that park, next to the courthouse. I noticed it again when I went to visit Merilee in jail. It's pretty public, but it has enough trees and bushes that I'm sure we can have some privacy there, too."

Molly grinned. "I like it. Is your phone all charged up so you can record?"

"I think so," Janet said. "Yours?"

"Yes. So between the two of us we should be able to record the confession and have our proof."

"I really hope for Merilee's sake and ours this works," Janet mumbled.

Molly tapped the number for the Flying B Ranch into her phone. "Hello? This is Molly Jones. I need to speak to Ray Boyd. Trust me, he'll want to take my call." There was a long pause before Molly spoke again. "Ray, this is Molly, Merilee's friend. Remember me?" There was another pause, then Molly said, "Good. You're gonna want to listen carefully. Janet and I have something that belongs to you. If you want it back, you're going to meet us in the park next to the courthouse in Shotgun City in an hour. You come alone, Ray, understand? If I see any of your minions hanging around, you won't get what you're looking for. I'm positive you don't want this particular item falling into the wrong hands, so you'll do exactly as I say. One hour in the park by the courthouse."

Molly hung up the phone and Janet let out a little scream. "Well, what did he say?"

"That's the crazy thing," Molly said. "He never even asked me what, specifically, we have. He may assume we're bringing him the will. He tried to bluster and bully, but you heard me shoot him down."

Janet bit her lip. "I'm still not convinced this is a good idea. Maybe we should call Bartlett."

"This is the best chance we've got to get a confession out of Ray. If Bartlett gets involved, the other cops could notice, and some of them are working for Ray. The whole plan could backfire."

Molly looked at Janet. "All we have to do is be smart and push Ray in the right direction and stroke his ego enough to get him to admit to drugging June and hitting her over the head. We're going to act impressed by everything he says. People who think they're untouchable love nothing more than telling others how smart they are. You know that."

"I do," Janet acknowledged as she pulled into a parking spot on the courthouse square near the park. "Smart thinking, giving us an hour to get set up."

Molly nodded. "I wanted to give us some time to get our bearings and find the best location. We want to be visible obviously, but we also need to make sure none of Ray's goons show up, jump us, and take the map."

"I guess it's too late to take a self-defense class?" Janet joked.

"That's not a bad idea," Molly said. "You know, in case we find ourselves in a position like this again."

"No way!" Janet exclaimed. "This is a one-shot deal. I don't want to become an amateur sleuth."

Molly laughed and unbuckled her seatbelt. "It's good you parked the Bug so close, just in case we need to make a run for it."

Janet groaned. "You aren't helping my anxiety."

Molly laid her hand on Janet's arm. "We can do this. We're going to get Merilee out of jail and get justice for June."

Chapter 17 *(by Linda Rawlins)*

Ray hung up the phone and stared at the fireplace. His hands curled into fists at his sides.

"Bad news?" Gibbs asked as he finished pouring whiskey into a crystal tumbler sitting on the wooden bar. He turned back to Ray who was now standing near the fire with a poker.

"No, I think it's good news, all in all. Apparently, we're going to have to play a little game to get what I need."

"What does that mean?" Gibbs asked as he drank from the glass.

"Merilee's friends think they're smarter than they are and apparently they're under the impression I'm a stupid man." Ray threw the poker, and it fell to the side of the fireplace with a clatter. "I didn't get where I am today without having a plan. I still have a plan and things are starting to come together. No one's getting in my way at this point, especially those two silly little girls."

Gibbs downed the rest of his whiskey and slapped his glass back on the bar. "So what do we have to do?"

Ray turned around. "What I need you to do is round up Jax and Ricky and get them into the truck. I'll be there in a minute and we're going for a little ride. I'll let you know what the plan is when we're on our way. I have to make a quick call to the Shotgun police station before we leave."

Ten minutes later, Ray jumped into the truck and started driving down the dusty lane that led out of the ranch. Jax, sitting in the back seat with Ricky, watched clouds of dust rise around the vehicle as they bounced up and down. He had to reach up and plant one hand on the roof of the cab and the other on the door to brace himself. He looked at Ricky with his eyebrows raised.

When they hit the paved roadway, Ray looked at the boys in the rearview mirror. "We're on our way to a park next to the courthouse and I'm going to tell you what you're going to do," he said. "You haven't gotten it right yet, so this is your last chance. I'm tired of all the drama, and we're going to end it now. Once I get what I need, you two will get paid and move on." Ray glanced into the mirror again to see if the boys were listening. Satisfied they were, he laid out his plan.

The truck didn't bounce as much on the paved road, and now that he didn't have to hold on for dear life, Jax had no problem keeping a hand in his jacket pocket. He was thankful he'd learned to thumb-text his phone keyboard without having to watch every letter. Ray would *not* have been happy if he'd known Jax was texting someone. Hoping his message would reach its destination, he clicked the send button and gave Ray his complete attention.

A short time later, Ray pulled the truck into a parking spot near some high bushes at the edge of the park and slipped out of the driver's seat without turning back. He walked into the middle of the park where the two women were waiting.

Using the bushes as cover, Gibbs quietly slid out the passenger-side door, just as Ray had told him to, leaving it unlatched to make sure he didn't draw any attention from the noise. Having the door open would also help in case they needed to make a quick getaway. Following Ray's directions, Gibbs waited to make sure the two boys stood near the bushes where they wouldn't be seen. Once satisfied that they were in position, he scurried off to find the girls' car. He was told to look for either a red bug or an old Civic with a busted taillight—the one Janet had driven to the ranch when Jax had kidnapped her. Gibbs's job was to disable the engine.

"Well, well. If it isn't Nancy Drew and friend," Ray said with an arrogant laugh as he approached Janet and Molly. "You two really should learn to mind your own business."

"The only business we have is proving Merilee didn't kill her mom," Molly said.

"Good luck with that," Ray said with a smirk. His face became cold as he eyed each of the girls. "I'm tired of playing games." Extending his arm he said, "Give me what you found so we can all go home."

Janet stared at the man. She couldn't believe she could detest him even more than she had back when they'd worked on the ranch. "We have a problem here, Ray."

"And exactly what would that be?" He kept his hands in his pockets and a frown on his grizzled face.

"Merilee's in jail for killing June," Molly said, taking a step closer to Ray. "Her mother. Your sister?"

"I know my family history. I don't need a smart-mouthed girl telling me about it."

"And we know Merilee could never hurt her mother. She's been upset and grieving ever since June died."

"And funny thing, Ray," Janet said. "You, on the other hand, don't seem too broken up that your sister was murdered. Most family members would ask a lot of questions. They'd try to find answers and understand how something so tragic could happen."

Ray looked at his watch, then scanned the park. "What's your point?"

Janet took a deep breath. "We found your map. And we know all the stories . . . About Sam Bass. And his hideout. And where it might be located. And what might be hidden there."

"Then you know why I need to make sure no one else can stake a claim."

"So it's true?" Molly asked. "The money? The robbery? The legend?"

Ray laughed. "Yes, it's true. As a matter of fact, one of my stupid ranch hands found Bass's gun belt and had no idea what he was holding."

Nearby, an exasperated grunt could be heard, coming from a bush.

"We've also been very impressed with your pull at the police station," Molly went on.

"You're a powerful man, Ray," Janet added. "Couldn't you see your way clear to getting Merilee out of jail for us?"

"Merilee for the map," offered Molly.

"Oh, you're going to see Merilee very, very soon. Now, give it here before I get mad," Ray said with a scowl.

Janet and Molly looked at each other, then Molly gave Janet a little nod. "You're really a pretty amazing guy," she said, smiling at Ray, even though it made her stomach turn to do so. "The way you just took what you wanted. The way everyone else thought those old stories were just tall tales. But you always knew they were true. How did you do that, Ray?"

"And the way you just cleared the path to what you were after," Janet added, forcing herself to sound impressed. "I admire a man who does whatever it takes."

"The thing is, we get why you had to kill June." Molly inwardly cringed at her own words. But she knew she had to play to Ray's gigantic ego.

Ray was clearly listening. His hardened expression had suddenly turned to one of utter surprise. "Well, sometimes a man has to do what he has to do," he said.

"Absolutely," said Molly. "Too bad every man isn't as forthright as you. I mean, when I think of how you just got rid of June and changed the will . . . It, well, it gives me chills." Molly actually did have chills at the moment—because her skin was crawling.

"Well, it was—" Ray eyed Molly. Then Janet. Then a gleam of suspicion sprung into his eyes and a slow grin spread across his face. "You almost had me there," he said in a very low voice.

Molly felt a knot in her stomach and raised on her toes, ready to jump if need be.

Ray finally stepped back and surprising them, let out a loud belly laugh.

Janet glanced at Molly, not sure what to do next.

Ray took off his Stetson and bent to swipe the ground. When he stood back up, his face had turned as hard as stone again. "I don't know if you're wearing a wire or what's going on, but I ain't that stupid. As far as I'm concerned, I didn't do anything to anybody."

He took Janet by the arm and she winced in pain. Molly started to move forward, but Ray raised the gun he had in his jacket pocket and pointed it at her. "Stop now or your friend is dead."

Molly froze as Ray shifted the gun to Janet's belly, making sure it was hidden inside her coat, so no one could see it.

"Like I said, I'm tired of playing games." Ray gave a sharp whistle, and in seconds, Gibbs, Jax, and Ricky all ran out from the bushes. Gibbs put his arm around Molly's shoulders and Ray did the same to Janet. "Let's take a walk to my truck. We're going to take a little ride. I'd suggest you keep your mouths shut and cooperate."

Janet and Molly complied. They were being held so tightly, they couldn't squirm and their captors were ready to muffle any potential screams.

"But first, how about a surprise before we leave for our little party?" Ray said, stopping next to the police cruiser that was parked near the Flying B truck. "Didn't I tell you you'd see Merilee soon?"

Sitting in the back of the police cruiser was Merilee, her face near the window, fear in her eyes. Her shoulders were pulled back, her arms behind her. She was handcuffed. Molly and Janet recognized the officer at the wheel: Officer Scott, whom they'd met at the station the same day they'd met Bartlett. It seemed so long ago now.

"Time to get this party started," said Ray. "By the end of tonight, all my problems will be gone. Thing is, bad things happen to friends who try to break someone out of prison." Ray gave the officer a wave, and then shoved Janet into the back seat of the truck. Gibbs did the same to Molly. Jax and Ricky sat on either side, and Gibbs and Ray jumped into the front seat.

With a howl and a hoot, Ray started the engine and pulled away. The police cruiser followed.

No one noticed that behind them, a powerful black truck, scratched on the sides, followed at a safe distance. The three inside were intent on staying close to their target, waiting for the right time to strike.

Chapter 18 *(by Randy Burkhead)*

The truck finally finished bumping its way down the road to the Flying B, the police cruiser pulling in right behind it. The ride had been totally silent. Once they arrived, the girls were quickly ushered into the living room. Several old-style wooden chairs were clustered near the fireplace, and Ray motioned for the girls to sit.

"Get out," Ray said to the four men standing behind him after taking a seat facing the girls. Jax raised an eyebrow in defiance but turned to leave when Gibbs put a hand on his shoulder.

Ray and the three girls stared at each other for a long moment.

"Where's my map?" Ray was eerily calm and had an authority to his voice that made it clear why he was the one in charge of his gang of roughnecks.

Merilee, unmoved, said, "I don't know what you're talking about."

"Oh I think you do by now, Merilee. I know all about how you and Janet here got some time together in the slammer, although I doubt you were in on their little plan to trick me." Ray turned his head to eye Molly and Janet.

So someone *had* been listening the night Janet visited Merilee in jail—although back then, none of them knew about the map, and Merilee was actually telling Ray the truth.

"I'll only say this one more time," Ray growled. "Where's my map?"

Janet was surprised when Molly boldly said, "It's in a safe place. You won't be getting it until we get Merilee cleared of all those bogus charges."

Ray was unconvinced, and let out a long sigh. Suddenly, he exploded up from the chair and was inches away from Molly's face, "I will not play your game. Tell me or I'll . . ."

He didn't get to finish his threat. Janet practically screamed out, "The library!"

Ray looked at her and smiled, "Please continue."

"We hid it in the library here in Shotgun City. It's in a book of old maps." Janet stared at the floor. She couldn't bring herself to look at her two friends.

"What maps?" Ray asked.

"Old maps of Packsaddle Mountain and the area around it," Janet said. "That's how we knew we'd remember where we hid it—because your map covered that area too."

Ray smirked and left them, practically flying out of the room. It wasn't long before Gibbs could be heard telling Ricky to get to work out in the pasture with the other ranch hands, and Jax to stay and stand guard. Then Gibbs and Officer Scott walked through the room and out the door together, and the house became quiet.

"I can remember so many happy times in this room," Merilee said, looking around.

"Me too," said Molly, smiling faintly.

Janet, who was still looking guiltily at the floor, had begun to cry.

Molly and Merilee hurried to sit down next to her and put comforting hands on her shoulders. She finally looked up and wiped the tears from her face. "Remember that time we tried to roast marshmallows in the fireplace, and they caught on fire?" Janet tried to smile and gave a little laugh.

"The fire alarm went off, and Mom came running," said Merilee, tears springing to her eyes as well.

"Someday, you're going to get this ranch back," said Molly, looking at Merilee. "And you're going to bring it back to life. And we'll have good times here again."

"Mom would like that," said Merilee. "And this is only a short drive from our neighborhood in Dallas." Merilee's whole demeanor changed as she thought about the possibilities. "We could come out here anytime we want. I could find a trustworthy foreman. Hire some honest help. This could be our weekend place, maybe. Just imagine! Someday, maybe our kids will play together here—just like we did."

The three friends continued to reminisce about the good times in the past, and dream about the good times to come. They knew they were being watched, so they avoided too much talk about their current situation—except to agree quietly that they'd look for a chance to escape and stick together no matter what. After about an hour, the door to the living room flew open and Ray stormed in, fit to be tied.

"I'm not one for wild goose chases," he said in a menacing voice, glowering at the girls. "Now you're going to tell me where that map is, or you're going to be very, very sorry."

He was so upset he forgot all about closing the door or keeping his voice down—and didn't notice that Jax had followed him into the room.

The more Ray ranted, the more unhinged he became. Gibbs and Officer Scott rushed into the room to hear what the commotion was about. When Ray's tirade went on and on, Jax started to say something to reason with Ray, but he didn't get more than a word out before Ray shoved him out of the way—hard enough to knock him to the floor. Jax broke his fall with his right hand

and gave out a yelp. As he got to his feet, he was holding his arm as if it might be broken.

Ray asked the girls about the map again and again, and each time they insisted it was in the book of maps at the library, he seemed to get angrier.

"It's time you told me the truth!" he yelled, and walked closer to the girls.

"Uh, Ray?" Gibbs said. "Don't forget about our uh. . . company that's coming soon."

Ray finally stopped yelling and became aware for the first time that he had an audience.

"Cuff them," he said angrily. Officer Scott instantly moved to put the girls in handcuffs. "None of these girls leaves this room. And when I get back, I expect you to tell me the truth about the location of that map!" Ray slammed his Stetson onto his head. "And then we'll get on to the will!" He stormed out, the other men following him.

Several minutes passed, and the room grew quiet again.

"I'm so, so sorry," Molly said softly. "This was all my fault. What a stupid plan. I underestimated Ray."

"It's not your fault Molly," said Janet. "It could never be your fault that Ray Boyd is a monster."

"Is this the same plan Ray mentioned earlier?" asked Merilee. "Tell me all about that."

Janet explained their plan to use the map and will as leverage to trick Ray into self-incrimination and prove Merilee's innocence.

"Why didn't you get Denny or Bartlett to help?" Merilee asked. "You put yourselves in serious danger for me."

"We were afraid to trust Bartlett," said Molly. "And I thought Denny would slow things down—

and maybe you'd meet with an *accident* like your mother did if we didn't hurry."

Merilee sniffed and yanked at her handcuffs. "I wish I could hug you. I love you both. You did all this to help me. No one could have better friends."

"I love you both too," the other two said almost in unison and each managed a smile.

Merilee swallowed hard. "If anything, this is all my fault. I made a mess of my own life, then let things get heated with Mom. If I hadn't made it so easy for Ray to frame me, none of this would have happened. I should've been honest with both of you about what was going on with me."

Janet shook her head. "It's not your fault either, Merilee. You had a problem and you were brave enough to overcome it. You're amazingly strong."

"Don't lose hope. We're going to get out of this mess," Merilee said. "I promise."

Meanwhile Jax, listening from the other side of the door, wrapped a bandage around his arm, hoping it wasn't broken. He downed some aspirin for the pain. As he stood guard, listening to the girls' teary exchange, he knew he'd definitely had more than enough of Ray Boyd. Sure, Jax needed money—and Ray paid well. But somewhere, there was a line that even Jax wasn't willing to cross. These girls didn't deserve this kind of treatment, and the more Jax saw and heard, the surer he was that he'd been working for a lowlife all along. His cell phone buzzed. Justine again. Good.

Earlier in the day, when Ray had given orders about how they were going to go to the park and trap Merilee's friends, Jax had had his concerns. So he'd texted Justine—who'd given him quite a scolding after the night he'd kidnapped Janet—and told her to come to the park as well, and to stay out of sight. If anything went wrong, and Ray succeeded in getting Molly and Janet into his truck, Justine was to follow them, and then, once on the ranch, to wait out of sight just up the road.

Jax hadn't been sure what he was going to do at the time, but he knew now, and he was glad to know Justine was waiting nearby. Jax texted her again now, telling her to wait until dark and to be ready for a signal when it was time to make their escape. He knew he'd have to be careful, but if he could get the girls safely off the ranch, he might just be able to redeem himself and get out of this whole mess. Those girls had something Ray wanted badly, and if it was something Ray wanted, then it was something Jax needed to get to first.

While Jax waited for night to fall—knowing that eventually, Gibbs would go to bed and the ranch would be quiet, he thought about this business with the map. Why was Ray so obsessed about a map? Maybe it had something to do with oil? Oil was big money in Texas.

He heard Ray return from wherever it was he'd gone. Jax peered into the kitchen and saw that Ray had sat down for dinner. Once Stella, the housekeeper, had set out the food, Ray grumbled that she didn't need to trouble with cleaning the kitchen or doing any other chores that evening.

After Stella left and Ray finished eating, he came back into the living room and poked at the fireplace while Jax and the girls looked on, waiting. He said nothing, but the way the firelight was dancing on his face was spine-chilling. Eventually, Gibbs came in as well, took a few drinks of whiskey, eyed the girls, then said he was turning in and left.

"Jax," Ray finally called out to him as the fire began to die out. "You have the first shift. I'll tell Ricky to come in and take the second. In the morning, you take your pay and I never want to see or hear from you again. Do you understand?"

Jax started to speak but stopped himself, took a deep breath to steady his nerves, and simply said, "Yes, sir."

Jax breathed a sigh of relief when Ray clomped out of the room. He waited thirty long minutes, straining to hear any sound coming from Ray's bedroom at the back of the house. When it had been silent for a while, he left his spot across the room and approached the girls.

"Don't worry. You can trust me," he whispered.

"Why should we trust you?" Merilee whispered back.

"He's okay," Janet said. When this met with looks from both Molly and Merilee, Janet said, "He's made mistakes. But I trust him."

"We have to go now," Jax said. "Justine's here. She's waiting up the road."

Jax took out his key and fumbled to unlock the handcuffs. They all moved quietly through the house and stepped onto the front porch.

They froze when they saw the form of man sitting in one of the rockers in the darkness. They were pretty sure it was Gibbs. He appeared to be asleep—or passed out, if the cloud of lingering whiskey fumes was any indication.

Jax motioned them to continue forward, and they crept down the stairs and onto the drive. He breathed a sigh of relief when they'd cleared the last step.

Suddenly, a shot rang out. All four of them turned to see a wobbly Gibbs trying to hold his gun steady.

"Run!" Jax yelled.

Unable to keep the fleeing people in his sights, Gibbs tried to run after them but tripped on the steps.

Unfortunately, the danger wasn't just from him. The house lights were coming on as they all took off running down the drive.

A pair of headlights sprang to life in the distance as the shot rang out. As they got closer Jax yelled, "Now, Justine!" into the darkness.

Molly recognized the truck instantly by the scratches on the sides, and felt a little wave of guilt as the rear cab door flung open for them and Bartlett's voice could be heard, hollering over the wind, "Are you all okay?"

"We're okay!" Janet called back, reaching up and accepting a hand into the truck. "What are you doing in there?"

He didn't get a chance to answer, because as soon as the door was closed, Justine put the pedal to the metal and flew down the bumpy road, all of them hanging onto whatever they could for dear life. Once they hit the highway, Bartlett flipped on the light in the cab revealing Justine at the wheel and Denzel in the passenger's seat.

"Denny?" Molly said, stunned to see her brother.

"Justine called me and I called Denny," Bartlett said.

"And *you* called Justine, right?" Janet said, turning to Jax, who was sitting meekly in the corner, still holding his arm. When he nodded, Janet smiled at him. "I knew you'd do the right thing eventually. Thank you."

Jax beamed and turned as red as a beet.

"So Jeremy's letting you borrow his truck?" asked Molly, smiling broadly at Justine.

"We had a little chat, and he says I can drive it anytime now," said Justine with a wink.

Even in a king cab, it was still a bit cramped with five adults in the backseat. As soon as it was safe to pull over, Molly climbed into the front with her brother to make some space.

"I should've called you," she said, laying a hand on Denny's arm. "And Officer Bartlett, you too. This whole thing has been so crazy, we forgot that sometimes we need to have faith in people and ask for help."

"Live and learn," Denny said, shaking his head at his little sister. "You're safe now. That's all I care about."

"So what do we do now?" Merilee asked. "How can we put an end to Ray's schemes once and for all?"

"We had some leverage with that map," said Molly regretfully. "But I guess it's gone now."

"And it's not like we can go to the police—present company accepted," said Merilee. "Half the cops in Shotgun City are in Ray's pocket."

"Did somebody say something about a map?" Justine said with a smile. All heads turned to look at her. "When Jax called me and told me to hightail it over to Shotgun before you met Ray at the park, I saw you two go into the library. I watched you hide the map. Then when you went back outside, I grabbed it. Figured you might need it."

"So that's why Ray was so angry! He really couldn't find the map. That's fantastic!" said Molly. "Let's make a plan—one that actually works."

In the dim cab light, Merilee squinted at the map, spreading it open as best she could in the space available. "Uncle Ray thinks Sam Bass's hideout is on the ranch. I guarantee that's what's going on here," said Merilee. "He's been looking for it pretty much his whole life. He's been taking notes—"

"And look at the map," said Janet pointing to a spot with a lot of writing. "He's narrowed it down to Packsaddle Mountain. There are all sorts of notes written in around it—most of them illegible. But there's something there about the gun belt he apparently found a few days ago. Didn't he say it had belonged to Sam Bass, the outlaw?"

"That son of a—" Jax shifted in his seat. "*I* found that belt out by where the herd broke through the fence in the south pasture. Not Ray. It was the same place the boys had found a bunch of dirty old coins—and Ray took them and gave them like ten bucks apiece. I knew that sounded too good to be true! You're telling me those were valuable?"

"Very valuable," said Bartlett. "Sam Bass's stash is legendary around here."

Jax's eyes lit up like a kid in a candy store. This was just like one of those Old West movies. Outlaws. Secret hideouts. Gold.

"I never believed those old stories," said Merilee. "But if my mother is dead because of that gold . . . Ray Boyd had better never get a penny of it."

Chapter 19 *(by Cheryl Davis)*

Ray stormed out of the house, letting the front door swing and slam into the chair that Gibbs had been sitting in. Gibbs lay at the bottom of the stairs, wailing in pain, his gun on the ground next to him and a lingering haze of whiskey surrounding him.

"How could you let them escape?" Ray spat out the words, while he pulled his suspenders up over his shoulders. "I'm surrounded by imbeciles and drunks." He pulled a Colt .45 from his belt and loaded it. Each click of the cylinder added to his confidence.

Gibbs let out another groan from where he still lay on the ground.

"Never ask a boy to do a man's job." Ray looked as far down the drive as he could see, to where the red taillights of the black truck zipped away from the ranch.

He turned to Gibbs, "Now get your filthy, whiskey-drenched, good-for-nothing self up off the ground. It's time you made amends for your incompetence."

Gibbs stood slowly, heavily favoring his right foot while he dusted dirt from his pants. "It was Jax; he helped them escape," he said, wincing from the pain that shot up his left leg.

"I knew I couldn't trust that boy," Ray said, staring toward the empty road. "Round up the other boys. I know right where they're headed, and I know the shortcut to beat them there." Ray looked down and spat in the dirt, missing the tip of Gibbs's boot by an inch.

"I'm on it," said Gibbs, and he turned and limped off toward the bunkhouse.

"I'll cut them off at Packsaddle Mountain—even without the map. I've studied it enough to know how to find what I'm looking for," Ray mumbled to himself as he stalked back toward the house.

The meeting he'd had a few hours earlier still lingered in his mind. Just remembering the details made his heart pound. Ray knew he needed that treasure for more reasons than greed. Gambling away a few coins was one thing, but getting in deep with the wrong people meant a payoff that Ray couldn't manage. He'd always been a gambler, but now fear seeped into his rusty old bones. Without the legendary treasure of Sam Bass, his debt would not be paid, and he'd not only lose the ranch, but most likely his life, too.

But the true gamblers of this world lived hard and fast, and Ray Boyd was no exception. He'd put the ranch up during a high stakes poker game. He'd thought he had it under control. He'd thought he couldn't lose. Some would call him arrogant for taking such a risk. Ray called it confident. Bold. But when he lost the game, he knew he had to find that treasure. *Fast.* Killing June and framing Merilee had been nothing short of necessity. Besides, they could never manage the Flying B the way he could. What did a couple of women know about taking care of a ranch, anyhow? He'd make it profitable, and he'd live out his days like an outlaw. He'd make the likes of Sam Bass seem like a pussycat.

Ray was so close to that gold now, he could almost taste it. And there was no way, after all of his work, and all of his searching, that he'd stand by and let someone else beat him to it.

The Flying B band of misfits loaded into the back of a beat-up pickup and followed Ray in his sleek red Ram truck—which he'd affectionately named

Darlin'. They rambled along the dusty road toward Packsaddle Mountain. By the time they arrived there, the full moon was high in the sky and illuminating the mountain like a silvery blanket. Ray sipped the thick-as-mud black coffee from his thermos while enjoying the view. If this were any ordinary night, he'd be snug in his bed, dreaming about the next day when he'd be out on horseback, inspecting the fields and checking the fence lines.

But this was no ordinary night.

Ray knew this land and the mountain like the back of his hand; he had a perfect spot in mind to hide out and lie in wait. He didn't know the exact location of the treasure but his gut instinct told him this was the general area. He had made notes in the margins of the map. He would wait, knowing Merilee and her friends would read those notes and follow the map, and then he'd catch them off guard and take the treasure for himself. The ranch boys were loaded up with various guns, and even though Ray didn't want any unnecessary bloodshed, the thought of an old-school Western shootout excited him.

Once he'd parked just off the road, Ray sauntered over to the driver's side of the old pickup. Gibbs looked rough, and was still complaining about the ankle he'd injured falling down the steps. Served him right.

"I want y'all to wait near Dead Man's Curve while I head up behind the great stone at the base of Packsaddle," Ray said. "My signal will be one loud shot. Once you hear that, you and the boys come running. Got it?"

Gibbs gave a grunt and a nod in the affirmative.

Ray shone his flashlight around at the rocky terrain, the ground dusty from a lack of rain. Packsaddle stood in the distance, the moonlight highlighting its beautiful curves. Years ago, the surrounding hills had been used as a film set, the backdrop so unique it took on many personalities depending on the weather and the season. Back in the old days, some of Ray's favorite Spaghetti Westerns were filmed right here. As a boy, he'd dreamed of being an extra in those movies—of riding a horse and shooting a gun. Now, he had a chance to act out his childhood fantasies. He was just missing the horse.

"I'm leaving Darlin' here," Ray said, patting his truck fondly. "I'll walk on ahead and wait for those meddlesome kids."

Gibbs shouted to the ruffians, "Out of the truck, you lot. Grab the guns, and we'll wait for Boss's signal."

Ray took one last swig of his coffee and set it back in the cup holder of the truck. Walking around to the tail end of Darlin', he yanked a large black duffle bag from the back of the cab, slung it over his shoulder, and began walking toward the foot of Packsaddle Mountain.

Chapter 20 *(by Lane Stone)*

"I think the back seat is asleep," Molly whispered to her brother, from her perch next to him in the front seat.

Denzel looked back and chuckled. "They all look pretty wiped out."

"I'm not asleep!" Merilee sat up straight and rubbed her eyes. "I've been thinking . . . Jax, you said Uncle Raymond paid some of the guys for those coins they found?"

"Yeah. So I'm told."

"So, if he has the loot, why does he need the map? He already has what he wants."

Molly smiled, glad her friend, the real Merilee, was back.

"There's a lot more out there," Bartlett said with a yawn. "Millions of dollars-worth. I read the Texas Rangers' file."

"Uh, Eric?" Janet looked closely at him. "You're not a Texas Ranger, are you? You said you were undercover, but did you mean you're undercover—as in, pretending to be a Shotgun City police officer?"

"Texas Ranger? Me?" Bartlett laughed. "No. You have to pay your dues by working in law enforcement for eight years before you can even apply to become a Ranger. But who knows? I've got the first four years under my belt, and I don't see myself staying with the force in Shotgun City forever." He smiled at Janet.

"He's been working undercover to get to the bottom of June's murder," Denzel said, a note of respect in his voice. "He's risked his life to do the right thing in the midst of a den of crooked cops. When this thing is solved, and Ray and his cronies are exposed, that whole department could finally be cleaned up."

"Molly, I can't see to drive with that map flapping around," Justine suddenly barked, reaching across the seat and pushing the map—which Molly had been studying—out of the way.

"Sorry, I didn't know it was blocking your view," Molly answered, and she folded the map and patted it down in her lap. She glanced in the rearview mirror and saw that Merilee and Janet were just as confused as she was by Justine's sudden wave of grumpiness. Molly gave a quick shrug. They were all exhausted, and anything she could do to help Justine keep the huge truck on the road and out of a ditch would be well worth it.

Jax leaned forward and gently, tentatively touched Justine's shoulder. "I can't believe you thought to get the map at the library. You're so . . ." His voice trailed off.

Molly glanced at Justine, but saw that her face remained blank at Jax's words. Her lips were pressed into a thin line, and her eyes never left the road. Something was definitely off with her mood.

"Yeah, we have the map and my uncle doesn't, thanks to you!" Merilee added.

At this, Justine nodded and gave a weak smile.

They drove on through the darkness in silence for a few more minutes, then Molly looked left and right out the truck windows. "It feels like we're driving in circles. Are we lost?"

Merilee leaned forward. "I was about to ask the same question. We're going to Packsaddle Mountain, right? I haven't been out there since I was a kid, but it seems like we should be there by now.

We need to get the coins and anything else Sam Bass left behind before Ray does."

"I thought it would be better to stay off the main roads," said Justine. "Like Eric said, we can't trust anyone at the Shotgun City police department. There could be an APB out for you. But don't worry: I had plenty of time to study the map while we were waiting for you back at the ranch house, and I know I can find Packsaddle." She began slowing the big truck down.

After they'd exited the ranch, Justine had managed to find one of the dirt roads that led back into the Flying B—but hundreds of acres away from the house. Now, the group was twisting and turning along the little roads that wove themselves through the property, using the full moon as their main source of light in the inky darkness.

"Oh! I know where we are now. Dead Man's Curve is about a mile ahead," Merilee said.

Justine pulled over to the shoulder. "I think we should walk from here. We need to get some distance between us and the truck."

Denzel had been quiet, but now he turned in his seat to face her. "Justine, your boyfriend does know we're out here in his truck, right?"

"Yes. Of course, he knows," she answered with a forced giggle.

"Let me guess. It has a vehicle recovery system installed, right?" Bartlett asked.

"Maybe. Probably. I don't know."

Janet looked around the interior and said, "A truck this expensive definitely does. Let's get out. Ray can't find the treasure because he doesn't have the map, but he might be able to find us."

"I'm not so sure about that," said Bartlett. "My guess is, Ray knows every detail of the map. He's studied it, and written all those notes on it. I'd be willing to bet he's memorized it."

"Then why was he so hell-bent on getting it from us?" Molly asked.

"Think about it, Mol," said Denzel. "What would happen if that map fell into hands other than Ray's?"

Light dawned in Molly's eyes, then in Janet's and Merilee's, too.

"And what do you suppose Ray is in a *very* big hurry to do right this minute, knowing we have the map?" Denzel looked at his sister, then back at the others.

"But he thinks we left the ranch, doesn't he?" Molly asked. "Surely he wouldn't think to search for us right here on his own property."

Denzel looked skeptical. "I think he'll guess exactly where we're headed," he said. "See, Ray's driven by greed—and he thinks everyone is like him. He's very likely to think that since we have the map, we're going after the treasure. That's what he'd do, after all."

"Oh, shoot," said Merilee, sitting back. "He's got to be high-tailing it out here too, then."

"We have to get a move on. I'll go hide the truck and walk back to you here," Justine said, shooing them out of the cab.

Jax, Janet, Merilee, Molly, Denny, and Bartlett all climbed out and stretched.

"When will I be able to feel my legs again?" Merilee groaned. "Hey, Justine—"

The rest of Merilee's sentence was drowned out by the spitting clang of gravel as Justine sped away from them.

"Justine!" Jax yelled, with a hurt look on his face.

"Where's she going? We have the map!" Janet said.

"Uh, no we don't," Molly said, squeezing her eyes shut in frustration. "She took it."

Chapter 21 *(by Carolyn Rowland)*

All eyes turned to Jax.

"Hey, I don't know what she's doing." Jax threw his hands up in exasperation.

"Justine's your ex-girlfriend," Janet said. "You probably know her better than the rest of us—even better than Merilee knows her. Would she seriously stab us all in the back?"

"Hey, I don't control her. And I never did really understand her."

Everyone turned to look at Merilee next.

"Sorry, guys," she said. "Justine is the kind of friend you meet up with for a fun Friday night. The truth is, I don't know what she's up to now. I hate to even think it, but maybe she just couldn't resist the temptation of going after that treasure herself."

Bartlett stepped forward. "This isn't helping us. We need a new plan." He turned to Molly. "You were staring at that map pretty hard, Molly. And Jax, you've worked out here on this part of the ranch before. Dead Man's Curve is still ahead of us and if my guess is right, some of Ray's men are probably already there, so we can't go that way. We need an alternate route. Any ideas?"

"There's some gullies that run the same path as the road," Jax said. "We rode across them a few days ago."

"Those are made from flood waters," Molly said. "They're like seasonal creeks that dry up when it hasn't rained for a while. They're not on the map because it'd be dangerous to use them. Water comes through from all over when it rains and you never know when there'll be a flash flood."

"If they're not on the map, that also means no one would expect us to be using them," Janet said.

"The gullies are deep. We could barely see over the sides when we were in them on horseback," Jax said.

"Sounds like we found our alternate route," said Janet.

Denzel and Bartlett both frowned.

"I'm not saying it's a great plan," Janet said. "Only that this might be a way for us to get past those guys waiting on us and get to Packsaddle without having to fight our way through."

"They do run the same way as the road and are at a lower elevation, so we might be able to slip by, even in the moonlight," Molly said. She looked at Jax then. "But can we truly trust you, Jax? You did work for Ray. This whole 'escape' might have been part of the plan, and you'll be reporting back to Ray."

"Right, and how would I report back? There's no cell service out here. And I don't have a walkie-talkie or anything like that. I'm as much in the dark as to why Justine left as you are. And I'm sick of Ray Boyd and everything he's about."

"Everyone, calm down," Bartlett said. "Here's how I see it. Our first two choices are, we stay here or walk until we can get cell service and call for help."

The girls shook their heads.

"Okay, then. The other options are, we walk forward into what's likely an ambush, or we try using the gully route to sneak by."

"Merilee, this place is your history. Your family land," Molly said, looking around. "This should be your decision."

Merilee didn't have to think about it for long. "I don't want to give up. I say we head for the gully."

"Okay, with about a mile to Dead Man's Curve and then another mile past it to Packsaddle, that's at least forty-five minutes in the gully, and we'll have to keep absolutely quiet. You ladies think you can be silent that long?" Bartlett asked.

Janet folded her arms across her chest, then released them as she laughed softly. "It'll be hard, but I think we can."

The others nodded their agreement.

"Everyone power down your phones and put them away. We don't have cell service anyway so they aren't useful and could put us in danger," Bartlett said.

With the phones off, the group took a minute to let their eyes adjust to the darkness.

Jax led them up the road a short distance, then veered left. When the land fell off into a shallow gully, he climbed down. Denzel and Bartlett followed and helped the girls down before Jax again took the lead on a path that headed almost parallel to the road. As they walked, the group went deeper into the gully.

The land gradually rose on their right until it was higher than their heads and they could no longer see the road. The moonlight gave them just enough light to pick their way along and avoid stumbles or twisted ankles on the rocky ground.

Suddenly, from the right, voices could be heard in the distance. Jax slowed his pace, and the group stuck close together, making sure not to talk. After another ten minutes of walking, they stopped.

"Did you all hear those voices back there?" Bartlett whispered.

Everyone nodded.

"I think that means we're past the curve. What do you think, Jax?"

"I'd say you're exactly right," said Jax. "I'd be willing to bet that's where Ray has the boys stationed. And I'm positive that was them we heard. I could hear Gibbs cussing."

Bartlett nodded. "You're all doing great so keep it up. The side walls are becoming lower and you'll need to bend down a bit so you aren't visible above them. We'll do that until it gets too low to go on, and then we'll climb out."

A low rumble reverberated across the ranch.

"Oh no, not thunder," Janet said.

"Of course it's thunder," whispered Molly with a little groan. "Nothing's gone right yet, so why should this? We need to move quickly in case there's rain—or even if there's been rain at some of the higher elevations around here."

"She's right," said Denzel. "We don't want to be in this gully if a surge of water comes down."

The string of bent-over walkers trudged on through the gully, stepping as carefully and as quickly as they could for a few more minutes.

As the first drops of rain fell, Jax looked back at the others and gave the signal to turn to the right. They all climbed up out of the gully and huddled together.

"Molly, you know the map best, and Merilee, you've been here before. And Jax, you were just out here on horseback," Bartlett said. "I can see hills ahead. Is that where we should go now?"

All three nodded.

"We still need to keep quiet," Denzel warned. "There's no cover out here so we can be seen if anyone is looking for us."

Janet, who had taken up the rear, suddenly stumbled and started to scream, but Bartlett quickly reached across and covered her mouth just in time to silence her. She gulped and pointed, horrified, at a large dark shape that had moved close behind her.

"It's just a cow," Jax whispered, struggling not to laugh.

Molly and Merilee giggled.

The cow chimed in with a loud, "Mooo."

"You wouldn't be laughing if you'd been nudged from behind," Janet said, catching her breath and trying not to laugh herself.

"Listen, if we're going to sneak around out here in the dark, we'll have to sober up," said Denzel.

"That's right," said Bartlett. "We need to be aware of what's before and behind us. Everyone needs to watch out for everyone else."

"The way I see it, the cows could be a help and a problem," said Jax. "We can use them as cover, but if they get spooked, they might stampede and plow over one or more of us—or call attention to our location. They also tend to bellow when they get spooked. Doesn't take much to get them started."

"Everyone keep a bit of distance and move slowly," said Bartlett. "Watch for holes and rocks."

"And cows," whispered Molly.

The rain began to pick up.

"Great. It's beginning to storm, we have armed ranch hands behind us and Ray in front of us, and now we have to watch out for cows, too. We just can't catch a break," Merilee said. "I was worried I wouldn't be able to prove my innocence, but now I'm not sure I'll survive long enough to even try!"

"This is no time to be a downer," said Molly, slinging an arm around her friend. "We're almost there and you've got all of us to help you. Forget about everything else. Ray is likely ahead of us somewhere and he doesn't know we don't have the map. We can still use that to our advantage."

"Unless Justine was headed his way. If he sees that she has the map, he won't need us at all, and all bets are off," Merilee said.

"We'll cross that bridge when we come to it," said Bartlett. "Right now, we need to get moving. Don't forget Denzel and I are here, and we're used to taking down bad guys." He stopped and peered into the darkness ahead of them. "I just saw a brief light—like a flame, about half a mile ahead. Could be someone smoking a cigarette. Does Ray smoke?"

"He sure does," Jax said. "Can't go for long without a light."

"The location's about right, distance-wise," Bartlett said. "Let's see if the cows will cooperate and cover our advance on him. I'd love to take him by surprise."

Chapter 22 *(by Karen Shughart)*

Justine realized, when she took the truck and left her friends, that they would think she'd betrayed them. But that was the farthest thing from her mind. She knew the group was entering into dangerous territory when dealing with Ray and his cohorts, and if he had killed June, he was entirely capable of killing the rest of them.

But Justine—unlike the others—had an ace up her sleeve, and as she pulled away from them, map in hand, she knew that if her plan worked, Ray would be arrested for June's death, Merilee's murder charge would be dropped, and the treasure of Sam Bass would be secure. Even now, Ray was lying in wait out here somewhere, expecting Merilee, Molly, and Janet to show up. He had no idea who he'd be dealing with.

Justine pulled the truck to the side of the dirt road, put it in park, and examined the map closely. If her instincts were correct, she knew just where she'd find Ray, and soon, he would no longer be a problem. Putting the truck in gear, she headed to the spot Ray had circled on the map. The outlaw Sam Bass had supposedly buried his treasure there, in a makeshift hideout built into a rocky cave, underneath the old rudimentary floorboards that had been laid down there. As the story went, when Bass heard that a posse was after him, he'd fled, leaving most of the loot behind.

Justine had heard the legend of Sam Bass since childhood—everyone who lived in the vicinity had. But one day, when Justine was ten and her brother, Rob, thirteen, their mother had taken them out to Packsaddle Mountain, had pointed out the hidden cave, and told them the true story about the outlaw—then she'd sworn them both to secrecy. It seemed Sam had been married to Justine and Rob's great-great-great grandmother, and before fleeing, had told his wife where the treasure was buried, giving her enough gold coins from his stash to support herself and their two small children for the rest of their lives. Then he'd disappeared—and was never heard from again.

The family lore about Sam had been handed down through generations, a cautionary tale of a misguided criminal—a sharp departure from the glorified Wild West stories that were told in town. When Justine had asked why her family had never tried to search for the treasure, she was told that they were embarrassed that their ancestor was an outlaw and wanted nothing to do with his ill-gotten gains.

Justine pulled back out onto the road, driving slowly toward her destination. She bent sideways, reached into her bag, and carefully slid out the gun she always carried. She took a deep breath. The story she'd tell Ray would be backed by the power and might of the gun she would not hesitate to use if circumstances called for it. She was confident she could hit her mark if need be; her daddy had taken her to target practice every week since she was seven.

Merilee, Janet, and Molly were decent people. True friends. June had been a good person, too. It was time to end this.

As Justine approached Packsaddle, she saw two trucks and an SUV. She recognized one truck as Ray's and smiled. She parked and pulled her cell phone from her purse. Good! Although weak, she had a signal, and she placed a call.

Ray was standing outside the cave with a shovel when she arrived. He looked up, puzzled, when he saw her get out of the truck and approach him. When he recognized her, he grinned, but his eyes were cold. Justine grinned back at him. If Ray thought he had the upper hand, he was gravely mistaken. He only knew Justine as one of his niece's friends. And he probably assumed he'd known everything there was to know about his sister June, too. But as he was about to learn, that was far from the truth.

Justine, on the other hand, knew the *whole* story. But she hadn't planned to do anything about it until she was driving back to Guitars and Cadillacs the night Molly and Janet had pulled her into this whole tangled mess with Merilee and June, and Ray. For Merilee's sake, Molly and Janet had been ready to put themselves in danger without a second thought. Now Justine felt convinced to do the same.

The part of the story even Merilee and Bartlett didn't know went back a few generations, to when Ray and June's mother, Tillie, had graduated from college and moved back to Shotgun City to work. That was when she'd started dating Justine's grandfather, Andy. After several months, Tillie had realized that while she cared about Andy, she was really in love with Thomas Boyd. The couple broke up—before Tillie knew she was pregnant. Things had moved quickly with Thomas, who loved Tillie back, and when she told him she was carrying Andy's child, he gladly offered to marry her and raise the baby as his own.

Tillie accepted, but both she and Thomas felt that the honorable thing to do was to tell Andy about the pregnancy. By then, Andy was dating a woman named Ellie Stevens and he told her about the baby; he wanted no secrets between them. Ellie appreciated his honesty and before long, they married, too, and had a daughter of their own, Adrienne.

A responsible young man, Andy offered to provide child support for little June. Tillie and Thomas refused, but Andy always kept an eye on June, just to make sure Thomas kept his promise to love and care for her, which he had.

Until recently, nobody else knew the secret of June's birth or that Justine's mother Adrienne and June were half-sisters—not to mention that Justine and Merilee were half-cousins. The two women had only learned about it a few years ago themselves. When Andy had developed a genetic heart condition, he and Ellie had informed their daughter, as well as Tillie and Thomas, who told June. Ray was not included in the conversation, because the families felt he had no need to know. Within a year Tillie died, and then a couple years later, Thomas.

Since then, June and Adrienne had become close friends and confidants. June told her sister that Thomas had rewritten his will after Tillie died, deeding The Flying B to her alone, and that she had revised her own will, leaving the property to Merilee if anything happened to her.

Thomas leaving the Flying B entirely to June hadn't sat well with Ray, of course, and June had confided this to Adrienne. Ray was furious. He said he was entitled to the ranch and threatened to harm June if she refused to deed it to him. He also threatened to harm Merilee unless June did as he asked.

Ray was becoming more volatile as each day passed, and June was understandably scared. But she also had no faith in the local police department, since Ray was tight with some of the men on the force.

June had gone so far as to write a letter to Adrienne, indicating that if something happened to her or Merilee, to look to Ray as the culprit. She had also had the forethought to tape one of the threatening conversations she'd had with Ray, put it on a flash drive, and include it, along with a copy of her dated, signed, and notarized will, with the letter. All of this came to Justine's mother, and through her, Justine had learned the whole story.

Justine walked toward the cave where Ray was standing with two other men. Beside them were several canvas duffle bags that looked full and heavy. She surmised they had managed to find and dig up the gold coins. The rising sun was bright, but even with her sunglasses on, Justine was unable to identify Ray's two companions.

Ray sauntered up to Justine. "Yet another one of Merilee's little friends," he said. "What are you doing here?"

"Thought I'd stop by and settle an old score," Justine said. "You killed June Mason and framed Merilee, and I have proof. I don't think you really want to be stealing that treasure."

Ray tried reasoning with her. "Justine, why should you care what I do? You know Merilee is pretty much a waste. Why risk your life to get involved in this? It's really none of your business, and I haven't a clue what treasure you're talking about. My friends and I are out here checking out some new pastureland for the cattle I just purchased in Wichita. Now why don't you mosey on back to town and let us finish up here."

"That's not going to happen, Ray. And if you want to know why I care, well, Shotgun is a small town. Turns out June was my aunt; Merilee is my cousin as well as a friend, and I care about getting justice for them both. Your game is up."

Ray looked shocked. "Cousin?" He scoffed. "What are you on about, Justine?"

"It's true. You and June are only *half*-siblings; her biological father is my granddad, but your father raised her as his own. The details are immaterial. Oh, and by the way, Sam Bass is *my* ancestor. Which is why I know for a fact that what's in those duffle bags over there are the gold coins he stole. He'd buried them out here at Packsaddle. And you finally rooted around long enough to find them, didn't you?"

Ray sputtered. "That's nothing but a pack of lies. My mother would never have been unfaithful to my father. She wasn't like that."

"You're correct, Ray. She was never unfaithful, nor was my grandfather. As I said, the details are immaterial. You'll have plenty of time to try and figure it all out in jail."

Ray regained his cocky composure. "I don't *care* about the details. Fact is, June changed her will and left the ranch—which you are now trespassing on, by the way—to me. Merilee will never inherit it. And Sam Bass and his treasure have nothing to do with my being out here today."

"You're a horrible liar, Ray. June had every right to inherit the Flying B, as your father intended, and it will go to Merilee—not you—now that June's gone. We all know you framed Merilee for June's murder," Justine continued. "And you know good and well you falsified that second will, leaving the ranch to you. But neither Thomas Boyd nor June ever wanted this beautiful land to fall into your selfish hands, and I'll bet that just irks you to no end, Ray." Justine leveled a steady gaze at him. "And just so you know, the proof that you killed

June is in a safe place protected by people much more powerful than you."

When Ray didn't believe her, Justine told him about the package June had sent to Adrienne—and about the recorded threats and the actual will.

Ray was beginning to look a little nervous. "Does Merilee know any of this?"

Justine glared at him. "Are you crazy? We all knew if you ever learned that my mother had evidence pointing to you as June's killer, you'd murder her too." She pointed the gun at Ray. "But you're not going to do that, are you, Ray?"

"If you're all so sure I killed June and forged a new will, why didn't you call the police and report all of these unfounded suspicions?"

"My mother did call them, the day after June died. But you know all about that, don't you? Mom very wisely withheld the information about the damning evidence June had sent her, because she wanted to make sure she could trust the police. All she said was that June had been a good friend and had confided in her about those threats you made, and that she was concerned you may have killed her, rather than her death being an accident.

"And surprise, surprise—your cronies in the department reassured her that despite your temper, they knew you weren't a killer, but just in case, they said they'd check to see where you were the night June died. That Officer Scott was very cordial when he called back and said that you were off in Wichita buying cattle, and lo and behold, your alibi checked out."

Justine took a step closer, the gun still pointed at Ray. "Now the way we figure it, either the police didn't check your alibi, or they just flat-out lied. June died in the afternoon, but my boyfriend,

Jeremy, and I saw you at Guitars and Cadillacs that very night, drunk, sitting at the bar. Ring a bell, Ray?" Justine scoffed. "You were nowhere near Wichita. And you should've known better than to go spouting off in public the way you did."

Ray shifted his stance a little and spit into the dirt.

"That's right, Ray," Justine continued. "We heard you bragging to the bartender. 'I've just become the owner of a big ranch, one of the biggest around these parts, and I'm going to be rich, too.' I called my mother and told her right away. So you see, Ray, the *police* were no help at all."

The greasy smile returned to Ray's face, and he strolled closer to Justine. "Put that gun down, Justine, if you know what's good for you. Go back to town and pretend this little meeting never happened."

Justine stood her ground. "I'm not leaving, Ray." Her hands were shaking, but she cocked the gun.

Ray laughed. "Little lady, you've just caused a heap of trouble for yourself. Do your friends or family know you're here?"

Justine stared at Ray, her eyes full of anger and fear.

"I thought not," Ray said. He motioned for the two men to come closer.

As they approached, Justine recognized them from the Shotgun Police Station. One was that crooked Officer Scott.

"See, Justine, I have friends in high places, too. I believe you've met Officer Scott here. And this is Officer Smith. Everyone will believe these fine, upstanding officers when they say they came out to the ranch to give me some advice about the best way to clear out these old tree stumps here to make a fine pasture out of this land." Ray put a boot on one of the tree stumps. "See, Officer Scott suggested I use dynamite." A slow smile spread on Ray's face. "I gave you the chance to leave, Justine, but since you refuse to go, you and that fancy truck will simply disappear, blown to bits in the dynamite blast." He sighed and shook his head. "What a pity."

Justine stood her ground, knowing she had to keep Ray talking, if only for a few minutes more. "There's something else you need to know, Ray," she said. "My dad's brother works for the state attorney general's office. Once it was clear the police department here wouldn't investigate June's death, we made copies of everything and turned it all over to them, and my understanding is that they now have enough evidence to indict you. So no matter what you do to me, they're coming for you, Ray. The game is up."

Ray scoffed. "You're bluffing, Justine. The AG's office never handles these types of cases. My bet is you've been bluffing all along and there's no evidence against me at all."

"I wouldn't bet on that if I were you, Ray. You know, things might go easier for you if you turn yourself in." Justine steadied the gun. "Or I could just shoot all three of you—and I will—if you come any closer. It would be self-defense, of course."

Ray rolled his eyes, chuckled, and glanced at his buddies. "Never gonna happen, Justine."

The three men walked menacingly toward her, hatred burning brightly in their eyes. Smith had removed a baton from his belt, and Scott had pulled his gun from its holster and pointed it at her.

Justine slowly backed toward Jeremy's truck. No one had answered the phone call she'd made earlier, but she'd left a message. Crossing her fingers, she hoped help was already on the way.

Chapter 23 *(by Elizabeth Jukes)*

"Of all the thingth I ever dreamed of doing ath a child, creeping around with cowth in the dark thure wathn't one of 'em," muttered Jax. "And are you thure we really need to talk like thith?"

"Yeth," whispered Bartlett.

In any other circumstance, it would've been laughable. Maybe someday, when this was all a distant memory, it would bring a smile and a chuckle. Bartlett, in an effort to ensure the group was not detected by Ray or his goons—and that no cows were unnecessarily spooked—had told them not to pronounce the letter 's' because that sound is known to carry further than other sounds. As a result, they were instructed to either stay as silent as possible or talk without making the 'sss' sound.

The group had been treading lightly, brushing against cows and gently nudging them so as to keep their "camouflage" heading in the direction of the lighter flame that Bartlett had spotted earlier. Jax's comment had been the first in a long, tense silence.

"I never knew cowth, moved tho thlowly," groaned Janet.

Molly couldn't decide whether she found it easy to stay silent because of the danger or because of the weirdness of speaking with a lisp. Whatever the reason, she and the others had stayed mostly silent and uncomfortably stooped over amongst the herd. The moon had been just bright enough that had anyone taken a good look at the cattle, any upright human figures among them could definitely be seen. Now, as the sky was lightening with the dawn, it was more imperative than ever that they stay low and quiet.

Twice during this trek Denzel had peered over the backs of the herd to determine who might be lying in wait with Ray. He knew it could be a trick of the moonlight, but he thought he could make out three people. They had safely passed the other crew back at Deadman's Curve and although Gibbs's voice had been recognized, they didn't know for sure how many others were there with him. But no matter how many of Ray's thugs were around Packsaddle Mountain, there was no doubt they would all be armed.

Merilee had been pondering the firearms count too, as well as Justine's inexplicable behavior. If Justine had joined forces with Ray, Merilee feared this whole operation was an exercise in futility. Maybe it was her aching back talking, but part of her just wanted to call the whole thing off. The threat of danger was just too great.

Bartlett, who'd been leading the group, had turned and was walking—crouching—back with a finger to his lips and a hand cupped to one ear. They were finally at their destination. Above the occasional lowing of the cattle, voices could be heard. Bartlett motioned them to get behind the nearby tumble of boulders the herd was passing. One by one, Bartlett, Denzel, Molly, Merilee, and Janet eased their way out of the herd and tucked in behind the boulders, where they all stretched out on the ground, resisting the urge to whoop with relief.

"I hear Uncle Ray," whispered Merilee as they tuned into the conversation coming from a cave in the side of the mountain.

"Yup," nodded Jax.

"I can see Officer Scott," growled Bartlett under his breath. "And the other guy is Officer Smith." He shook his head in disappointment at his fellow officers and exchanged a grim glance with Denzel.

The ongoing conversation of Ray and the two turncoats had turned to a discourse on the untold riches they'd just uncovered.

"Now what?" asked Molly.

"I'm going to inch around the curve here and see what I can see," whispered Bartlett.

"Are you sure?" asked Janet, horrified.

"We need to know the lay of the land," said Denzel.

Jax withdrew his gun from its holster. "I can cover you." He wasn't going to tell anyone else, but that was something he'd always wanted to say.

Molly picked up one of the many rocks around them. "Look at all these rocks. They should be good for something."

"Could we throw them? Create a diversion?" asked Merilee.

"Might could," nodded Bartlett. "Start gathering rocks. Make a few piles." He took a breath. He knew that if this whole thing went sideways, Denzel would ultimately cover Jax and do whatever it took to keep everyone else safe. Bartlett hoped that if he was spotted, the three robbers would be so drunk with greed that the appearance of a lone officer would only make them laugh. He was counting on them being the types to gloat first, shoot later. But most of all, he was hoping they were so distracted that he wouldn't be spied at all. Night had definitely come to a close, and the pearl gray of dawn was clarifying their surroundings—a circumstance not in their favor. No time left to waste.

Bartlett drew his gun. Jax and Denzel stood behind him. Janet, Merilee, and Molly continued to pile rocks. Then came the sound of a truck door banging shut.

Bartlett swore under his breath. He'd missed his chance.

The group heard Ray grunt, "What the—" and then call out, "Yet another of Merilee's little friends. What are you doing here?"

A female voice answered, and they all caught the tail end: "I don't think you really want to be stealing that treasure."

"Justine?" mouthed the friends to each other. They stopped piling rocks and listened intently as Justine dropped her bombshell.

"We're *cousins*?" gasped Merilee. "And I'm related to Sam Bass?" Then she began to cry as Ray—her own uncle, her flesh and blood—didn't even try to hide the fact that he'd murdered her mother in cold blood. "How could he?"

Molly and Janet each grabbed one of Merilee's hands, their eyes filling with tears as well.

"Molly, the rocks," said Denzel, pointing. "Get ready. This isn't going to end well for Justine if we don't make a move."

"What are you thinking?" asked Bartlett, roused from his momentary bewilderment as the implication of Justine's revelations hit home.

"This," said Denzel, and he quietly outlined his plan.

As Justine backed toward the truck, the men stepped closer to her. They were toying with her like a cat with a mouse because, as she well knew, they could kill her, hide her body out here, take the money, and run. They could be sitting on some beach in some foreign country by the time anyone found her. Should she shoot? Would the surprise of that give her a split-second to make a break for it?

As Justine took one more step back, her foot turned on a rock, causing her to lurch lopsidedly and heavily against the truck.

And with that everything erupted.

Jeremy's truck alarm roared to life. At the same time, rocks began pelting down on Ray and his fellow robbers, and soon Janet, Merilee, and Molly could be seen, popping out from a group of large boulders nearby.

"I'm more than happy to cast the first stone!" yelled Merilee, who was slinging rocks from atop one of the boulders using a pouch she'd made with her sweatshirt.

Bartlett, Denzel, and Jax shot at the ground beside each of the robbers' feet, making it very clear that they could hit or miss a target with impeccable accuracy.

"Drop your weapons!" commanded Bartlett.

Meanwhile, back at Deadman's Curve, the quiet and uneventful night had lulled Gibbs and the other ranch hands into a sense of sleepy ease. It had been the middle of the night when they'd arrived, after all, and Gibbs had had a few too many drinks back at the ranch.

When the rain started, Gibbs had helped himself to the front seat of Darlin,' stretching out so he could prop his injured ankle on the driver's armrest. Two of his cronies made themselves comfortable in the back seat and the other two took shelter in the old pick up. The rain didn't last long, but no one wanted to leave the comfort of the trucks, so they rolled down the windows and smoked a few cigarettes.

"Guess the boss should be along soon," said Gibbs, eyeing the lightening sky. "Must have done good since there's been no alarm."

No one answered.

Gibbs eased himself up and peered into the back seat to find the others sound asleep.

"Hey!" he shouted. "What do you think you're doing? Wake up!"

This was met with snorting and scuffling noises.

"Wasn't sleeping," someone said with a yawn.

"Just a light doze. Really."

"Whatever," answered Gibbs scornfully. "Ray should be back anytime. Go check on the others."

A shot suddenly rang out. Then another. And another.

Gibbs and his two passengers tumbled out of Darlin'.

"Move over!" Gibbs yelled at the guys in the old pickup as he yanked open the driver's side door. The other two clambered into the truck bed just as Gibbs squealed away.

"Didn't Ray say the signal would be *one* shot?" asked one of the guys in the cab.

"Yep," said Gibbs, a thin layer of sweat breaking out on his forehead.

"Something's happened."

"Yep."

In his rearview mirror, Gibbs caught sight of a cloud of dust rising in the distance behind them. Someone breaking camp early from the park down the road? The truck lurched over a large rock causing cursing in the back. Gibbs gripped the steering wheel and concentrated on the dirt road.

"Watch the road, will ya?" yelled one of the guys in the truck bed.

The other leaned over the side and shouted into the driver's window. "Do we know anyone in a little pink Honda?"

"A what?"

"A pink Honda?"

Gibbs could see it now too—coming up fast. The two in the cab craned their necks to get a look. Silly little car. Did whoever it was actually think they could pass him?

"Lean on the horn. It might warn the boss there's company coming," called one of the guys.

But before Gibbs could comply, all the guys started yelling and reaching for their guns.

The last thing Gibbs saw was a woman leaning out of the Honda's passenger side window, the gun in her hand raised, before he lost control of the truck as two tires were shot out from under them.

Justine stood against the side of Jeremy's truck. "Don't hit the truck!" she yelled over the yelps of Ray and his cohorts.

Ray and Officers Scott and Smith hadn't instantly thrown down their weapons at Bartlett's command. Bartlett, Denzel, and Jax, in an effort to stay out of the circle of pelleting stones, hadn't been able to move in fully. But when Justine shot at the ground behind them and the rain of rocks didn't let up, the weapons had finally hit the ground.

"Got you!" said Merilee as she jumped from her place atop the boulder. She strode over and stood in front of her uncle with her hands balled into fists. "I could absolutely punch you right now, but I don't want to lower myself to your disgusting level."

Bartlett, Denzel, and Jax moved in with their guns trained on the felons.

"Let's get you all cuffed up, shall we?" said Bartlett.

"Isn't that your car, Justine?" asked Merilee, pointing to the pink Honda that was now barreling toward them.

"It is. How did they get past Gibbs and the other guys?"

"Is that your boyfriend Jeremy driving?" asked Molly.

The sun was just peeking over the horizon behind them, shining light into the car.

"Yes. And that's my mom with him! I'd called him but he didn't answer. I wasn't sure if anyone would come."

The Honda ground to a halt with a crunching and spraying of small stones, and Jeremy leapt out. "Hey, Justine, are you okay?" But he was looking past her at his truck. "Is the truck all right?"

Getting out of her side of the car, Adrienne walked over to Justine and put her arms around her. "Is it done?" she whispered, hugging her daughter tightly.

Justine gulped and nodded squeezing her eyes tightly against the tears that were threatening to fall, the enormity of everything hitting her at once.

Adrienne stretched out an arm to Merilee pulling her into the family hug.

"Move over there," Bartlett ordered Ray, Scott, and Smith, pointing to the pile of boulders behind which the rescuers had hidden. "Sit down and don't move. Janet and Molly, I want you to keep some rocks close by and keep your eyes on them. You too Jax. Denzel and I will go and check on Gibbs and the other lot. Adrienne, with your sharpshooting skills, I'd appreciate your presence with us. Justine, would you be okay with that?"

"Sure. Do you want me to come too?"

Bartlett appraised the look on her face and Merilee's, and quietly said, "No, we're good."

"You sure you don't need my rock-throwing skills to come with you?" asked Janet.

Bartlett smiled. "Not this time."

"To save us time we'll take your car, okay, Justine?" said Denzel.

Justine nodded.

The three got in, Bartlett at the wheel. He spun the little car around and sped off.

Jeremy circled his truck slowly for about the third time, noting some new tiny pits and scratches in the paint. Jax stood beside his prisoners and watched him in disbelief.

"Jeremy," he called. "Come here."

Jeremy patted the truck's hood and stepped over.

"Yeah?"

"Don't you think you have something else to say to Justine?"

The three in the pink Honda didn't have far to go. With its two ruined tires, the old pickup truck had skidded a long way and smashed backwards into a cluster of scrubby trees.

Adrienne, Bartlett, and Denzel stepped out of the Honda slowly, guns poised and ready. But no threatening sounds could be heard from the wrecked truck. There was only muttering and moaning and quiet cursing. Gibbs was slumped motionless over the steering wheel.

"The glories of greed," sighed Adrienne.

Denzel reached through the window to check Gibbs's pulse and Bartlett dialed 9-1-1.

Chapter 24 *(by Leslie Stansfield)*

Early morning eased into what was, for late
autumn, a warm day. Duncan's Towing had long
since carted Gibbs's wrecked truck away. Molly
noticed Janet's pixie bangs were damp with sweat
that rolled into her baby blue eyes. Sitting on the
boulder next to her, Molly's box braids felt gritty
and sandy, and her glasses kept slipping down her
nose. Molly shoved them up one more time and
sighed as she looked around. The Shotgun City
police and the Texas Rangers were still combing the
area. Originally, there had been around twenty
officers in total. Now it was down to ten. Denzel had
left to help take in Ray and his crew, leaving Captain
Richard Hamer of the Texas Rangers in charge on
the ranch. Hamer commended Bartlett on his work,
and Molly—who had at first been a little swept away
by the handsome Captain Hamer—was glad to see
the young cop getting the credit he deserved. Maybe
he'd become a Texas Ranger sooner than he
imagined.

The cows seemed to be hanging around just to see
what would happen next. Molly would've thought
they'd have taken off, with all the activity, but their
intent brown eyes seemed to suggest that this was
the most interesting thing to have happened in the
back pasture in quite some time. Of course, Molly
mused, it was also the most interesting thing that had
happened to her in a long time, too.

Merilee came and sat down next to Molly and Janet. "Thanks for not giving up on me. I was scared to death. I can tell you that."

Janet's blue eyes widened. "It never even crossed our minds you could be guilty."

"We know you way too well for that," Molly chimed in. "We knew you'd never hurt your mother. She was your world. I'm just sorry you had to learn the awful truth about your uncle. That's got to hurt."

"At this moment, I'm just numb. It's all too much to take in. I mean, on one level, I suspected Ray. But now, knowing it for sure—knowing what my poor mother went through at the hands of her own brother . . ." Merilee shook her head sadly. But then she brightened a bit. "But I also found out I have family I never knew about. Justine and I have always liked each other, but who would ever have imagined that we're cousins?"

"*And* that you had Sam Bass's treasure on your property all along. Everyone thought that was just a myth. It's a real-life plot twist!" Molly said.

Merilee shook her head. "You know, if Uncle Ray's jacket hadn't ended up in my car, he could've gotten away with the whole thing."

"Well, not necessarily," Janet said. "Let's remember that Bartlett was already on to him. He was on the trail before we even got involved."

"When he was so cold to me at the jail, I couldn't believe it," Merilee said. "I thought he really believed I'd killed my mother. But then he slipped me a note, telling me not to give up hope. That's when I began to suspect something weird was going on. Remember, you both knew more than I did because I was sitting in jail." She sighed at the memory, but then a smile slowly spread across her face. "Molly, I'm starved. How about you whip us up some of your garlic hash browns when we get home?"

"Oh man, that sounds good," said Janet. "I've been trying to forget how hungry I am. I wish they'd just take us home."

"We've gone over our statements so many times, there isn't much more we can tell anyone," said Merilee. "I'm going to get some more water." She got up and headed toward a group of officers, and Adrienne and Justine joined her.

"Do you think Gibbs will make it?" Molly asked. "It sounds like his heart attack was pretty serious."

"It wouldn't surprise me if he's too mean to die," Janet said with a chuckle. "Meanwhile, the Shotgun police sure look bad in all of this. Bartlett was on his own, trying to figure out what was going on, but the rest of them . . ." She shook her head. "There's going to be a lot of fallout from this."

"Jax turned out to be a pretty good guy," Molly reflected. "Thank goodness there were lines he wasn't willing to cross." She nodded her head toward Justine. "I don't think she's over him. If Jax pulls it together, she might give him another chance. After all, he's a hero now. And that jerk Jeremy was more concerned about his truck than he was about Justine. Jax looks like a love-struck puppy every time he looks at her. I hope she'll give him another shot."

"Yeah," Janet agreed. "I had Justine pegged for a coward or a turncoat. When she took off like that, I wasn't sure whose side she was on, but I was sure it wasn't ours. Another miscalculation."

Suddenly, police radios began squawking and cell phones began ringing. A few of the cruisers took off in the direction of town. Some of the cows decided this was too much action for them and moved on.

Bartlett ran over to Janet and Molly, a look of alarm on his face. "Someone helped Ray escape.

Probably one of the guys from the ranch. He and Scott took off in another truck. They're unlikely to come here, but we're going to get you out of here, just to be safe."

He was just reaching to help Janet slide down from the boulder when there was a sudden gunshot, and Bartlett fell backward, holding his arm. More gunshots followed.

At that point, the few remaining stragglers among the cows had definitely had enough. They took off with gusto. Molly and Janet dropped off the boulder and onto the ground next to Bartlett. His arm was bleeding, but Molly realized he was okay when he grabbed his gun.

"Stay down," he ordered.

Molly looked around. Merilee, Justine, Adrienne, and one of the officers were ducking behind a squad car. She couldn't see Jax, but he had to be with them.

"Ray *just* got loose," Molly whispered. "Who's doing the shooting?"

As if he'd heard her, Ray's voice came from a few yards away. "Surprise, folks!" When he saw their startled faces, he added, "It helps to have someone on the inside to hold the dispatcher at gunpoint. Gave us time to sneak up on you. Y'all are making this way too easy."

"Give it up, Boyd!" Captain Hamer yelled. "There are too many of us. You can't win this."

"Oh, you'd be surprised how many I have on my side," Ray called back. "We just came to get what's ours. That, and a little revenge."

"Are you crazy?" Bartlett yelled to him. "What's the point? You'll never live to enjoy it. Drop the gun while you still have a chance of survival."

Molly looked around again. The gullies were behind them. Ray had come from another direction—more to the right. There was no vehicle in sight, so he must've walked a good distance. Molly eyed the two police vehicles and Adrienne's Honda. Would it be possible to get away, find Ray's truck, and slash the tires?

One of the officers got off a shot, but Ray just laughed. This was followed by more shots from police, and more laughter from Ray.

That was when Molly realized Ray wasn't the one doing the shooting. So then, why were the good guys shooting?

"Why are they shooting?" Molly whispered. "How do they know where Ray is?"

Bartlett smiled and winked. Janet and Molly exchanged looks of confusion.

There was another barrage of gunfire and this time, Ray howled in pain. "Son of a—" His voice was drowned in the sound of the shots ringing out.

Bartlett laughed. "That ladies, I believe, was the sound of Jax and Justine shooting up the bags of coins. Now Boyd can't move them. The bags are in tatters and the coins are, well, a bit scattered."

"Justine and Jax?" Molly asked. "But I just saw them behind that cruiser," she said, pointing.

"You *did* see them. And then someone covered them while they moved. I caught a glimpse of Jax's boot and Justine's shoe. That's when I figured it out what was going on."

At that moment, Molly heard a helicopter overhead. She shielded her eyes and looked up, and saw that it was a police helicopter.

"Just in time," Bartlett said with a smile.

"Last chance, Boyd," Hamer yelled. "You and your friends throw down your weapons and you live. You can't get the gold now. Might as well call it a day."

"Okay, okay," Ray shouted, then sneered in the direction of the cave. "Jax, you're a sneaky son-of-a-gun!"

"*Jingle all the way*," sang the group as Molly, Janet, and Bea toasted each other a month later, on Christmas Eve.

Molly thought this might just be the best Christmas Eve of her life. Bea had brought a feast fit for the Three Kings. Denzel had actually had to ask some friends of his to help bring it all over in their trucks. The Flying B Ranch had never looked more lovely, decked out with lights you could see all the way to Dallas.

Merilee and Jax, with a little time and a lot of hard work, had turned the ranch around, and put it on the road to becoming a real success. They'd also worked with the town and decorated twenty acres for people to drive through. They charged a fee, which would be donated to the local homeless shelter.

"My sweet girls, how amazing is this!" Bea cooed. "Merilee, you have done your mama proud. Never in her wildest dreams would she have thought all this possible."

Merilee smiled and wiped a tear from her eye. "I wish my mother had wound up with Bass's treasure instead of me. She would've loved being able to see her vision for the Flying B come true. Uncle Ray's gambling always sucked away any extra money, but now, just think of all the good we can do! I love having Justine and Adrienne in my life, too—not to mention my cousin Bartlett. I only wish my mother and Adrienne had gotten the chance to be close."

"Look who's here!" Denzel called from the hallway.

"Ho, ho, ho!" called Justine as she and Adrienne came into the kitchen.

"Wow, you are amazing, Bea," Adrienne said, marveling at the feast.

"Why, thank you," answered a beaming Bea. "How's Jax doing outside with the barbeque?"

"Great! He said it should be done soon. Denzel was going out the door as we came in. Those boys worked so hard, setting up the tents and picnic tables for tonight's feast and caroling. It's the talk of the town!" Justine said.

"Jax has been so amazing," Merilee said. "He's worked night and day with me to help turn this place around. I'm so glad he agreed to be my new ranch manager!"

"He's also making quite a name for himself in the Texas barbeque world," Bea added. "One day, we might see him on TV."

"I think seeing what laziness and greed can do to a person was a big wake-up call for him," Justine said.

"That and *love*," Janet added with a smile. "So glad you left Jeremy and his silly truck."

"Definitely!" Molly echoed.

Justine blushed. "I am sure they'll be very happy together. With the part of the treasure Merilee shared with mom and me, I bought him a new truck. It was good-bye and good riddance."

"I'll admit I didn't really like Jax as my daughter's beau in the beginning," Adrienne said. "But he's a new man, and he obviously loves Justine."

"Speaking of new loves," Molly said, turning to Janet, "where's Bartlett?"

Now it was Janet's turn to blush. "As soon as he gets off his shift, he'll be here. But Moll, I think it's too soon to call it love."

"Yeah, right," the other women said in unison.

"Well, with Ray behind bars for life and Gibbs in for the next ten years, I think we have lots to be merry about this Christmas," Adrienne said.

"The new year is looking bright, too," Merilee said. "Justine and I are going to open an ice cream shack here this summer. Jax and I are buying more dairy cows soon. It's more work than I ever imagined, but it's so much fun."

"The Flying B Dairy Farm," said Janet with a smile. "That has a nice ring to it."

"There you all are!" a voice from behind them said, and Captain Hamer walked in. He grinned at Molly and her heart fluttered.

"I'm going to go find the mistletoe," Merilee said in a gleeful whisper.

Of course, no Shotgun City Christmas Eve celebration would be complete without a visit from Santa, and Molly thought Huey Duncan made the best one ever. He arrived in a tow truck instead of a sleigh, but somehow, even that was perfect.

Bass's gold had changed all their lives and brought them together with a whole new group of friends and family—blessed them in ways they never could've imagined.

But Ray had had it all wrong, Molly mused. The *true* treasure was all of them together. And Ray had missed out on it because of his greed.

From jail to jingle bells, the journey had been pretty amazing.

Our Authors
(In Alphabetical Order)

Zaida Alfaro (*Chapter 13*) was born and raised in Miami, Florida. An avid reader of cozy mysteries and a singer-songwriter, she was inspired to combine her love of literature and music, and write her first cozy mystery, *The Last Note*. Zaida brings her love of Miami, Cuban culture, her family—and music—to readers of her novel. Check out Zaida at: www.zaidamusic.com.

Christian Belz (*Chapter 4*) has been a practicing architect in the Metro Detroit area for 33 years. This is his third time participating in the Cozy Cat Press group mystery. Christian loves solving puzzles and brings his real-life experiences to his mysteries and his main character, architect Ken Knoll. Known as Cannoli, Ken solves murders that plague his building projects. Contact him at www.KenKnollMystery.com

Lane Buckman (*Chapter 1*) is an author from Dallas, Texas. She loves mystery, romance, and comedy and always tries to work a reference to lip gloss or a tiara into her writing. Lane wrote chapters for the two previous group mysteries. Her cozy mystery *Tiara Trouble* is available on Amazon.

Dr. Randy Burkhead (*Chapter 18*) specializes in cybersecurity, and currently works as a security consultant. She is a regular writer on LinkedIn and has contributed to works of non-fiction and academia. This is her first published fiction contribution but she has multiple writing projects planned for the future.

Linda Clayton (*Chapter 7*) spent most of her adult life living in foreign countries, and this has given her plenty of fuel for her humorous Julia Greene Travel mysteries. She's been writing all her life but along the way she raised three kids, built and ran a fitness center, and had a successful career as a portrait painter. Contact Linda at: www.LindaSClayton.com

Cheryl Davis (*Chapter 19*) has served as a Lighting Artist for 20+ years in the animation industry. She has worked on films including *Mulan, Lilo and Stitch, Frozen,* and *Big Hero 6*. In 2017, Cheryl opened a bed and breakfast. She hopes to release her debut middle grade novel in 2021

Bart J. Gilbertson (*Chapter 3*) is the author of *Deathbed & Breakfast*, as well as an award-winning poem, "Mrs. Latimer Had a Fat Cat", and various published short stories, including, "Shout From a Rooftop". Bart is the father of two, and the grandfather of three. He currently resides in Nampa, ID, with his cat, Sophie.

Liz Graham (*Chapter 6*) graduated with a BA in Medieval History. She lives in St. John's Newfoundland where she renovates old houses. Liz is the author of the *Carmel McAlistair* Mystery series and the *Unlikely Heroine* series. Under the pen name E M Graham, she writes the fantasy series *The Witch Kin Chronicles*. Contact Liz at: http://www.LizGraham-Author.com.

Christina Hazelwood (*Chapter 10*) earned her BA in journalism, eventually garnering a career as a newspaper reporter and eventually an editor. Hailing from the 'Show-Me' state, Christina eventually landed in public relations and filmmaking. She also has a third career in real estate as a builder and rehabber.

Elizabeth Jukes (*Chapter 23*) earned a Journalism diploma followed by a Bachelor of Theology degree. *Pin It on a Dead Man* was the first cozy mystery she wrote and the first in her Dorothea Montgomery Mystery series. *A Taste of Northern Spies,* the second book in the series, was published in 2018 while a third book is percolating. Elizabeth lives in New York, Ontario.

Mary E. Koppel (*Chapter 9*) is a mother, Episcopal priest, and writer. She is the author of the Denise Reed Mystery series published by Cozy Cat Press, co-author of *Where God Hides Holiness,* and numerous other essays. Read Mary's blog at: https://reverendmomwriter.home.blog

Judy L. Murray (*Chapter 8*) is a Philadelphia real estate broker and restoration addict. She has worked enough with sellers, buyers, and agents to fill her head with many story ideas. Her first book, *Murder in the Master,* will be published by Level Best Books in 2021. Judy is a member of Sisters in Crime and Mystery Writers of America. www.judylmurraymysteries.com.

Joyce Oroz (*Chapter 2)* moved from painting portraits on canvas to painting on indoor and outdoor walls. Murals became her business and her obsession. Her Josephine Stuart Mystery series draws on these artistic skills. All twelve of the books are on Amazon. Joyce lives in Aromas, CA.

Rosie Pease *(Chapter 11)* is a native Rhode Islander but has also lived in Vermont, New York, and Ohio. She uses the places she's visited as inspiration for the settings of her cozy mysteries. When she's not writing, Rosie likes hanging out with her family. Contact her at: www.amazon.com/author/rosiepease.

Dr. Emma Pivato *(Chapter15)* is a retired academic and psychologist. She has seven Claire Burke mysteries in print along with a personal memoir, and she's working on a specialty cookbook— *Gourmet Puree: What to Do if You Can't Chew!* Emma's main preoccupation is her daughter, Alexis, and how to create a life for a child born with multiple profound disabilities.

Linda Rawlins *(Chapter 17)* is an American writer best known for her Misty Point Mystery series, including *Misty Manor, Misty Point, Misty Winter* and *Misty Treasure.* She graduated from medical school and established her career in medicine. She is the 2020 President of Sisters in Crime— Central NJ. You can contact her at: www.lindarawlins.com

Carolyn Rowland *(Chapter 21)* writes historical fiction, Sci-Fi, fantasy, and the Haunted City mystery series. Her short fiction can be seen in upcoming volumes of *Fiction River*, *Pulphouse Magazine,* and various anthologies. She has won several short story contests. You can follow Carolyn at: www.carowland.com.

Shawn Shallow *(Chapter 12)* authors the Hannah Sparrow Mystery series which features a sleuth who uncovers crimes tied to pivotal historical events. Excerpts from some of Shawn's work have been featured on the History Channel and several radio talk shows. Shawn currently works in banking, and lectures on maritime history for US cruise lines. He lives with his wife Margaret in Birmingham, AL.

Jenna St. James *(Chapter 16)* writes in different genres. She currently has three cozy series: Ryli Sinclair mysteries, Sullivan Sisters mysteries, and Copper Cove mysteries. Her paranormal series with four other authors is A Witch in Time. Her romantic comedy series is Trinity Falls. Contact her at: https://jennastjames.com

Karen Shughart *(Chapter 22)* is the author of two non-fiction books and has worked as an editor, publicist, photojournalist, teacher, and non-profit executive. Her cozy mysteries in the Edmund DeCleryk series include *Murder in the Museum* and *Murder in the Cemetery*. She is working on book three. You can contact Karen at: https://www.karenshughart.com.

Leslie Stansfield *(Chapter 24)* is the author of the Madeline's Teahouse mystery series. Leslie is a graduate of the University of Hartford and recently received her Masters' degree from the University of Phoenix in Educational Leadership. She is a math tutor and Christian Education Director of her church.

Lane Stone *(Chapter 20)* lives in Alexandria, Virginia, and Lewes, Delaware. Lane writes the Tiara Investigations Mystery series and the Pet Palace Mystery series. Lane enjoys traveling and volunteering for good causes. She has a post-graduate certificate in Antiquities Theft and Art Crime. Contact her at www.LaneStoneBooks.com.

Jennifer Vido *(Chapter 5)* has written three books in the Piper O'Donnell Mystery series. She also writes a bi-weekly column on FreshFiction.com. As a board member and spokesperson for the Arthritis Foundation, she's been featured by Lifetime Television, *Redbook, The New York Times, The Baltimore Sun,* and *Arthritis Today.* Jennifer lives near Baltimore with her family. Contact her at www.JenniferVido.com.

Diane Weiner *(Chapter 14)* is a mother of four and a veteran public school teacher. She has previously published several music education articles as well as a doctoral dissertation but finds writing fiction to be much more fun. She currently resides in South Florida with her family. When not writing, Diane enjoys long-distance running.

Made in the USA
Las Vegas, NV
24 March 2022

46251498R00108